D1491222

PIXIL·LATED

PIXIE-LATED

NEWBORN PIXIE COZY MYSTERY BOOK THREE

WILLOW MASON

ISBN: 979-8-6300-2755-9

CHAPTER ONE

*M*uffin pushed at the potion bottle until it teetered on the edge of oblivion.

"Do you mind?" I asked, shoving it back into the centre of the kitchen table. "That's the only sample we have."

"But it wants to be on the floor." The kitten's whisper was mesmerising—soft and seductive. "Can't you feel that?"

"It wants to be in the pantry," Brody said, snatching the bottle and holding it to the light. "Now, so long as everybody remembers not to drink the strange blue liquid, it'll be fine in there."

Muffin's face collapsed as my cousin pushed the concoction onto a high shelf and pulled the door closed.

"Are you really planning to use the potion on Lucas?" Muffin asked.

"Not until I know for sure what's inside it. That's why I've invited Darla Quincey over this morning. Rosie recommended her."

"A first-tier witch?" Brody's eyebrows nearly disappeared into his hairline. "My, we're getting fancy, aren't we?"

"I think the recommendation had more to do with her experience in chemistry than what level of witchcraft she's achieved." The words sounded sure when they came out of my mouth, but a wriggle of doubt remained.

Since my arrival in Oakleaf Glade and introduction with the world of supernaturals, I'd only had one encounter with a witch. My neighbour, Hazel. Although she'd only been third tier, she'd also turned out to be a murderer and thief. Not a great representative for the group.

"You'll be in safe hands," Muffin assured me as though reading my mind. "Darla works in a compounding pharmacy that serves the entire South Island and never had a single mistake. Someone with her eye for detail and knowledge of chemical structures will work out if it's safe."

"Or we could just put a few drops in Lucas's cuppa the next time he pays one of his unnecessary home visits," Brody suggested with a rakish smile. "See how it goes."

"And be up on a criminal charge if it goes terribly," I answered, giving him a poke in the ribs. "Aren't you going to be late to work?"

"Nope. But I am running late for a job interview."

My mouth fell open. "When did this happen?" Another thought occurred to me. "Oh my gosh. You haven't been fired from the Tavern café, have you? I'm happy to boycott them if that's the case, only…"

Only, their cheesecake was divine and no other restaurant in town understood the art of a triple-deep-frying their chips to achieve maximum crunchiness.

"Don't worry. No one's been fired. I'm just sick of working weird hours for minimum wage."

"Where's the interview?" Muffin asked, tackling what should probably have been my first question.

"And what's the job?" I left off giving Brody the third degree to answer the door—our regular early morning delivery from the town's best bakery. "Here you go." I unwrapped a triple chocolate muffin and passed it across to my kitten before taking another for myself. Pet ownership had greatly increased my sugar consumption.

"I'll tell you if I get it," Brody said, instantly becoming a man of mystery. After helping himself to an apple muffin topped with a slice of tasty cheddar

3

aged enough to put hairs on his chest, he waved goodbye and shot out the door.

"Perhaps he's lined up a job at the bakery?" Muffin said in a voice full of hope. "Since you wouldn't even try."

"They didn't have an opening," I reminded her, pressing my finger against the muffin wrapper to pick up each delectable crumb. "But I should probably look for something. The jar in the pantry might refill itself now, but it doesn't mean it will forever."

The money jar my great aunt had somehow magicked into providing a steady stream of crumpled notes had been a delightful find. However, after spending three weeks lounging around at home, interspersed with doses of crime-solving weirdness, I could feel my natural work ethic reasserting itself. A break was nice, but I needed to find something industrious on which to spend my time.

When I first arrived, there'd been talk of an opening at the sewing store in town—a position that would have suited my skills admirably. Unfortunately, the ad was long gone from the area's tiny recruitment section.

"The library needs an assistant." Muffin stretched and jumped from the table, running straight for a bright patch of morning sun. "Although I'm not sure if the role is paid."

"I'm happy to volunteer my services for now."

Especially since I had no idea of how to be a librarian except for shushing. That I could do like a champion. "Once Darla's been and gone, I might head along there."

"It'll be nice to have this place all to myself during the day." Muffin stretched out full-length and smacked her lips before rolling over to expose her belly to the light.

"Didn't realise I was cramping your style," I said while transferring the remaining bakery items into an old biscuit tin. It wouldn't fool any guests for long, considering each treat was wrapped in the bakery's name-branded wrapping paper, but it seemed fancier than the paper bag.

"Who's that?" Muffin jumped to her feet, back arching and her fur standing on end. She skittered away from the door, eyes wide with horror.

My pulse sped up until I saw Darla's friendly face peering through the window. I waved and opened the front door, standing back as she and a man entered.

"This is Reggie Barr, my partner," Darla said, waving towards her friend. "He's just here for moral support."

"And because I'm desperately nosy," Reggie added with a good-natured grin, white teeth flashing through the disguise of a dense moustache and beard. His chestnut hair was fashioned into short dreads, ending just above his shoulders, and he wore a pair of old-style dungarees, carefully worn and torn in all the fashionable places.

"Get out," Muffin said, rearing on her back legs and hissing. "There's no place for your sort around here."

"Muffin!" I picked her up, feeling her muscles tense, fighting against the move. "Don't be so rude." I mean, the guy was obviously a hipster, but that was no reason to kick him out.

The kitten struggled out of my arms, backing into the lounge.

"I'm so sorry," I said, shaking my head as Muffin retreated into the far corner, almost out of sight. "She's usually welcoming to strangers."

"No worries." Reggie clapped his hands together, beaming. "Since I'm just tagging along for the ride, I can wait in the car if you prefer."

"We'll be in and out in five minutes," Darla said, putting her hand on Reggie's arm to stop him going. "Then your familiar can have the run of the house again."

"The potion I'm worried about is in here," I said, trying to ignore the prickles running up and down my spine. Whatever Muffin had experienced on sight, I now seemed to be getting a low-level dose. With a shiver, I grabbed the bottle off the high shelf and thrust it towards Darla.

She pulled out a pair of thick, horn-rimmed glasses

and peered intently at the bottle. "This came from a monster hunter?"

"A vampire stole it from Blake Stone, the man who—"

"I know who he was," Darla said with a wave of her hand, cutting me off. "The ratbag ended up getting exactly what he deserved."

A stake in the heart seemed a bit overboard to me, but I kept my mouth buttoned. An aura of certainty radiated off the witch, leaving me feeling even more out of my depth than usual.

"I should be able to handle this in my lab," she said, glancing up from the blue potion. "I can reverse engineer the exact recipe to find out what we're dealing with. Even if it won't work for your friend, it'll give us a better idea of what the monster hunters are up to."

She pulled the cork out and took a tentative sniff of the contents. "Hm. There's something sharp in there." Darla turned to her partner, lifting one eyebrow. "Maybe a smidgeon of Hemlock?"

Reggie's nose twitched with such vigour I was afraid he was about to sneeze. "Valerian, salvia, mugwort, and wild dagga at a minimum." He tilted his head to one side, eyes closed as he sniffed more deeply. "There're so many hallucinogens in the mix I'm not surprised the hunters see things when they take it."

"You can get all those ingredients just from smelling?" I was as surprised as I was impressed. "Can I take you down to our local KFC and get the list of secret herbs and spices?"

Darla laughed as she pushed the cork back in to seal the bottle. "Are you a fried chicken connoisseur? Because Reggie's services don't come cheap."

"We're more into muffins," a small voice called out from the connecting doorway. Muffin sat on her hind legs, licking her paw and patting the fur around her ears. "But don't bother getting us a recipe. Elisa has trouble following instructions."

"That might be true, but it's still uncalled for." I gave her a puzzled frown. The small kitten was just as much of an extrovert as I was, and even her snark was usually good-tempered. Something was awry.

"I probably should've called first," Darla said as she stowed the potion in her enormous handbag. "But it's been so long since I had a familiar, I tend to forget about them."

When I continued to stare at her in confusion, she laughed and gestured towards Reggie. "My friend here's a werewolf. Probably why your kitten hated him on sight. But what he lacks in feline appeal he makes up for with his sensitive nostrils."

Darla continued speaking, but the words turned to static buzzing in my ears. A werewolf? I shot a sympathetic glance at Muffin, deciding next time I should follow her advice, and never mind the rudeness.

"No need to look so worried," Reggie said, beaming again. This time, his smile opened so wide his tongue hung out. "I'm harmless. Even if the full moon's due tomorrow night, I don't hunt pixies."

"But do you hunt kittens?"

"Nah," the man said, ducking his head to avoid my gaze. "I'm so out of shape nothing needs to worry." He patted his belly, which didn't look the slightest bit flabby to me. "It'll take a year's worth of effort at the gym before I can look forward to fresh rabbit again."

"Yeah, you slowpoke." Darla gave him an adoring smile before turning back to me. "It'll take me at least a few hours to break down the exact ingredients. Then we can run a test on a willing subject to find out what the formula does to human perception."

"You test on humans?" I shifted my weight from one foot to the other.

"Well, the only alternative is animals and, apart from familiars who can already see supernaturals, they're not easy to understand. Have you ever tried to interview a guinea pig about their experiences?" Darla rolled her eyes. "You can't get a word of sense out of them."

I giggled at the image of a witch interrogating a wee animal. "Point taken. What if it hurts the subjects?"

"I won't feed it to anybody unless I think it's safe. I'm a witch, not a scoundrel."

"Though some days it's hard to know the difference," Reggie whispered to me, earning himself an elbow to the chest from his beloved.

"Somebody's coming," Muffin called out in a worried voice. "Were you expecting anyone? It will do my reputation irreparable harm if I'm caught in the company of a dog."

"Wolf," Reggie growled while I walked to the door, frowning out the side window. Usually, it was Muffin who told me who strangers were since she knew practically everyone in town.

But she didn't know the two people standing on the footpath, frowning at their phones before glancing at the front of my house. I threw the door wide open, my happiness overriding the deep concern surging through my body.

"Mum!"

CHAPTER TWO

"If we're in the way, let us know," my mother said, poking her head into every downstairs room while I trailed along behind her. "We can always get a room at the pub in town if you don't have space. I'd hate to impose on you."

"Stop it. I'll hear no such thing." I closed each door my mother opened, trying to remember if there was anything magical on display that shouldn't be. Since my mother would have pixie blood in her veins, even if it wasn't dominant, she might catch an eyeful she wasn't prepared for. "You're welcome to stay as long as you want. In fact, I'll take you upstairs right now and show you the spare room."

"Nonsense. You sit down and have a rest. Me and Ben will have a quick tour around the rest of the house, then we'll pop into town and organise a motel."

"But I want you to stay here," I protested, falling into my mother's passive-aggressive dance with the ease born of old habit. "I *insist* that you stay here."

"No. I won't hear of it." My mother opened the back door and stared into the yard, frowning at the creepers growing over the back fence. "Ben! Did we pack the clippers? That ivy will grow so heavy it'll pull the wall down, then you'll have much closer acquaintance with your neighbours."

Ben Neal gave me an apologetic smile. "Sorry, love. I told her to give you fair warning we were coming, but she got a bee in her bonnet about the trip and wouldn't listen."

If one of my faults was being nosy, my mother's was complete ignorance of any feedback received through her ears. Along with that ran a deep streak of stubbornness, which annoyed me no end because I'd inherited the exact same trait.

"Would you like a cup of tea?" I asked, giving up and deciding I might as well wait out the inspection in the peace of the kitchen. "We've got a nice array of muffins, too, if you're hungry."

"Sounds great."

Ben nodded to the other guests as he settled in at the table. Although he'd never officially done the deed and married my mother, he still insisted on introducing himself as my stepfather.

"We should probably go," Darla said with a glance

at her watch. "I've got a long list of medicines to prepare and ship out before the last courier pickup."

"You're a chemist?" Ben's eyes lit up, and he grabbed the witch's hand, forcing her to take a seat. "Excellent. My doctor diagnosed me with sciatica but doesn't have a clue on how to manage the pain. What would you recommend?"

"My dad suffered from that," Reggie said with sympathy. "Got so bad he could hardly work."

"It's a trial." Ben's eyes twinkled. The only thing he loved more than comparing war wounds was detailing their effect on his daily life. How my mother coped with knowing every twinge and ache, all day long, I couldn't imagine.

"Elisa! Do you have a man living here?"

With a guilty gasp, I ran to the foot of the stairs and peered upwards into my mother's angry face. "It's not what you think," I said, scampering up the steps. "He's not a man, he's Brody."

Muffin sniggered, no doubt storing up that titbit for a later revelation.

"If that's meant to mean something, I don't know what it is." My mother perched her hands on her hips and glared.

"Leave her alone, love," Ben called out. "If she wants to shack up with a man, it's only because you and I gave her a shining example."

"He's my cousin." I reached the top of the stairs and

hugged my mother, ignoring the thunderous expression. "There's no chance of funny business. He just can't afford his own place at the moment, so I told him he was welcome to stay."

"What cousin?" My mother refused to be mollified. "I don't recall any cousins with that name. I hope you've not let a stranger take advantage of your hospitality. You're such a generous soul, you must pay extra special attention. Otherwise, you'll end up destitute."

"I'm careful."

"Hm. Well, this Brody better be able to recite our family history backwards and forwards, otherwise, he can look for another place to stay tonight."

"You can't kick out my roommate." I mirrored my mother's body language, shoving my hands onto my hips with my chin jutting out. "And what family history? You haven't told me anything about our family."

"Of course, I have. You know Uncle Pete and Aunt Ginny."

"Wow. Okay. And are we now pretending that's the entire family?"

My mother's face went dull with shock, but she soon rallied. "It's the only part we care about. Now, where's this room? Ben needs to rest after the long drive up here."

"I'm okay," Ben called out from downstairs. "Why

don't you come down and join us in a cup of tea. They've got muffins."

"They soon won't if you keep guzzling them," Muffin said, followed by a string of what might have been kitten expletives. "Elisa, can you get your family under control? This isn't acceptable behaviour."

I rolled my eyes at my familiar, remembering too late my mother couldn't hear the kitten so thought I was dissing her.

"That's how you treat your mother now?"

With a sigh, I closed my eyes and remembered how nice our daily phone calls had been. Since moving out of my childhood home a few years ago, I'd forgotten how tiring it could be to spend time with my mother in person. Over the phone she was lovely.

Deciding it would be best to extricate myself rather than continue sparring, I walked back to the kitchen.

Downstairs, Ben sat, happy as a clam with a cup of tea in one hand and the remains of a peach and custard muffin in the other. A distraught kitten sat opposite him while Darla and Reggie stood, declining offers from my quasi stepfather that he had no right to make.

"We should probably get going," Darla repeated as soon as I walked into the room.

"Nonsense," Ben insisted, pulling his chair around to face the witch. "There's plenty of time left in the day. Tell me how you know our Lisey."

15

Ugh. How I hated the nickname. What was so difficult about pronouncing three syllables? "That's not my name."

"She loves it, really. Little Lisey. I've called her that since she was only this high." Ben's hand hovered about two feet off the floor. Considering he'd begun dating my mother when I was at high school, his approximation of my height missed a good three and a half feet.

"Where's this Bodie?" my mother demanded, stopping to plaster a kiss on the side of Ben's face.

"Brody and he's at a job interview at the moment."

"He doesn't have a job!" Mum's face collapsed in horror. "Oh, no. No. No. This won't do at all."

Muffin snuffled in a way that sounded suspiciously close to muffled laughter. I helped myself to another treat from the tin, quelling her amusement with a large bite. "Brody has a job at the Tavern Café. He's just looking for something better."

"And what are you doing? Have you found something yet?"

"I've got an interview lined up at the library," I merrily fibbed, thinking what my mother didn't know couldn't hurt her.

"What do you do?" My mum stared straight at Darla, unfazed at the fact she was demanding answers from a stranger.

"I'm a compounding chemist."

"Now, see." Mum pointed to Darla in case I'd somehow missed the fact she was sitting there. "That's a real job. Perhaps you should take some time to work out what you want from life and train up while you've got the energy."

Visions of report cards where the alphabet began at C then went downhill strayed into my mind. I'd struggled through secondary school and now my mother believed I could handle a tertiary education. Fat chance.

"What room are we staying in?" Ben asked, leaning back and patting his fed belly. His expression was so like Muffin's after she'd had a feed that I couldn't help but smile. "I'll fetch the bags from the car."

"How long are you staying?"

"Why? Is there a problem? What else are you hiding? Are you a punk now? Is that why you've coloured your beautiful hair?"

I tucked a strand behind my ear and smiled guiltily. In the rush of her arrival, I'd forgotten there were a lot more changes going on than just my roommate or the inherited house.

"Just asking so I can buy more groceries when I'm shopping today."

My mother hooked an eyebrow up, nostrils flaring as she scanned my face. "Okay, then. We don't have any formal plans. I've just been worried, what with your discoveries of dead bodies everywhere. Thought I'd check in and see what's going on."

"The killer was found and sorted," Reggie said, easing himself into a chair and earning a scowl from Darla. "We're usually a peaceful place. Ask anyone."

"It's not like I stumble across bodies every day, Mum." I reached over and hugged her. "And you're welcome to stay as long as you like. You know that."

She bit her lower lip, suddenly appearing closer in age to me.

"Come on, Kayla," Ben said, giving her a pat on the rear. "Once I've sorted out the luggage, we can take a nice stroll around town and see what this place is like for ourselves."

"Fine." She threw out her arms. "Just call me an overreacting busybody. Show us this spare room and we can work things out from there. But remember, I'm still happy for us to stay somewhere else. Don't want to be a burden."

My insides squirmed at her protestations, but I kept my mouth shut. No matter what I said, it would go down the wrong way.

Although my mother would already have seen my messy bedroom, I closed the door as I reached the landing. Brody's attic room was up a short staircase to the side of my room and I walked straight past, unlocking a side door and showing Mum and Ben inside.

"I think this used to be the servant's quarters," I explained, opening the shutters. "There's a bathroom through the connecting door there"—I pointed—"and the sliding door here opens onto a balcony."

Mum ventured outside, gripping the railing and shaking it firmly before heading back indoors. "It doesn't seem safe. Have you got a building inspection?"

"No, not yet."

"These old places can be death traps, you know."

I nodded. Considering the house was self-repairing, I wasn't worried in the slightest, but that explanation was at the end of a long road I didn't want to venture down.

"We'll just keep the door locked," Ben said, doing the deed. He stood back and twirled around, his eyes taking in everything. "This is far grander than anything I was expecting. If you sell this place, you'll make a mint."

"I have no plans to sell," I blurted as Muffin's face turned thunderous. "This is just perfect."

Darla sidled into the room, her protestations she must go overturned by the temptation of snooping. Reggie pressed in behind, his nostrils flaring as he sniffed the air.

"It's musty," I apologised, opening a window. "As far as I know, Great Aunt Esmerelda didn't use this part of the house at all."

"She certainly didn't." Muffin strode across the room and jumped on the bed, raising a cloud of dust. "Do you feel the atmosphere? It's downright oppressive."

Between the expected and unexpected guests, I hadn't noticed, but after Muffin drew my attention to it, I had to agree. The feeling of disuse was one thing, but I struggled to catch my breath in the heavy air. Unusual and unpleasant.

"There's something hidden away over here," Reggie said, tugging at an inset closet door. Locked. He sniffed along the tiny gap between the door and the jamb, growing more excited with each breath. "It smells old and wonderful." A line of drool oozed from the side of his mouth, turning the denim of his overalls inky blue where it landed.

"Use your magic," Muffin said, forgetting her antipathy towards Reggie as she joined him in clawing at the door.

Hunching my shoulder to hide my actions from Mum, I scratched a small helping of pixie dust from my head and visualised a key. With a soft blow, the smoke travelled out in a thin line, then reversed direction, leading me towards my bedroom.

It hung in a small cloud above my keyring before dissipating into the surrounding air.

"Good point," I muttered under my breath, walking back to the spare room and flicking through the keys until I found one the right size. "Stand back, Reggie."

The werewolf took an obedient step away, catching Muffin around the midriff and lifting her clear when she paid no attention. I slotted the key into the door and turned it, trying to ignore the flutter of anticipation in my belly.

"Voila!" I flung the door open. A broom propped in the corner began a slow tumble forward and I caught it, staring inside the cupboard with disappointment. "What smells so exciting about a broom closet?"

But Reggie was already inside, pressing at the corners. "There's a false wall back here," he said, giving it a punch.

I winced and glanced at Muffin. "Perhaps we should use a crowbar or something?"

"No, I've got it." Reggie gave the wall another punch, hitting it so hard with his knuckles my hand ached in sympathy. One more knock and the wood splintered, giving him access to insert a hand into the gap.

Although my feet wanted to walk backward, I forced myself nearer to the closet, staring into the gloomy shadows behind the fake backboard. "Can you see what's in there?"

"Bones." Reggie sniffed, then pulled at the collapsing wood, revealing a skeleton.

It stood upright, with all the pieces in their proper

places. A faint glow emanated from it, so dim it wouldn't be visible except for being stored in a dark cupboard.

"I love bones," the werewolf growled, snuffling closer. "And these have been here for decades, getting ripe."

Mum held a hand to her mouth, then ran to the bathroom. The sounds of her being sick made me gag in sympathy.

Reggie stretched out a finger and caressed a clavicle with unrestrained longing. The bones shrieked, as if in pain, and collapsed into a pile on the floor, puffing up a cloud of sparkling dust.

"Perhaps we should just settle for sleeping on the couch," Ben said, scuffing his feet and casting concerned glances everywhere. "Seems like this room's already taken."

CHAPTER THREE

"This is the skeleton of a pixie," Officer Syd Abney told me hours later, once the pathologist had carefully removed the bones from their hiding place and documented everything he needed.

"How can you tell?"

"The remnants of pink hair and the sharp chin. If the remains still had cartilage, you'd also have seen pointed ears." He shuffled his feet back and forth, glancing over his shoulder when Ben told a joke outside that earned a round of laughter. "There's also pixie dust all over the floor. Whoever sealed the body up inside, did it while it was still intact."

My stomach heaved, and I held a hand up to forestall any more forthcoming information. "That's impossible. The stench of a rotting corpse isn't something a few boards can seal in."

"But a magic spell might do it. At least until nothing but the bones were left."

Muffin trotted into the lounge, making a beeline for my lap. "I think your mother has sorted out new accommodation. Reggie is bringing around a large tent and they'll weather the elements outside."

"That's ridiculous." I frowned at my mother and Ben as though they'd found a body on purpose just to spite my hospitality. "They can use my room and I'll sleep on the couch. It's not like they're going to stay here for months on end."

"Better grab Reggie before he heads off," Muffin warned. "He seems very enthusiastic."

"He's basically an overgrown dog," I muttered. "Enthusiasm is his natural state."

Muffin smiled in appreciation before closing her eyes and falling deeply asleep. I envied her the ability. For myself, I forecast a long night ahead with every creak in the floorboards turning into a roaming skeleton.

"How long has the body been in here?"

"Hard to tell. Once the pathologist examines the bones in more detail, he might hazard a guess. We'll check whatever features we can determine against the missing person register."

"Not even a guess?"

Syd rubbed the back of his neck and sighed. "I just hope it was whoever owned the place before Esmerelda. I was fond of the old duck and would hate to think she hid a body in the walls."

I nudged Muffin, wanting to ask her questions, but she was either solidly asleep or feigning the state to avoid me.

"How many people go missing from Oakleaf Glade each year?" I asked. "Surely there can't be that many."

"Lots of people go missing everywhere, all the time." Syd closed his notebook and tucked it away in his breast pocket. "Oakleaf Glade isn't any different. If the pathologist can narrow it down to a year, we'll have a good chance of working it out. Any wider a gap and we might never identify the victim."

"The body," I corrected. "We don't know they're a victim of anything."

"Fair enough." Syd sauntered towards the door, keeping a close eye on the position of everyone outside. "But then you've got to answer why someone would board up a body in their spare room if the lady died of natural causes. Can you think of a reason?"

"Give me time and maybe I'll come up with something." I pressed my lips together. "But no, I can't think of anything on the spot."

"In the meantime, keep the spare room locked.

Until we can work out if we're dealing with a crime scene, it'll be best to restrict the foot traffic."

"Believe me. Nobody is going in that room." I shuddered. "I've half a mind to sell the place just so I don't have to think of it ever again."

"Elisa!" Rosie waved and jumped off her bicycle, dropping it near the front gate. "How're you doing, you poor love? We heard all about it."

Posey reached me sooner, wrapping her arms around me in a bear hug. "What a terrible experience." She stepped back, cupping my face in her hands. "I swear this town is usually a lot nicer to live in."

"I'm starting to think you're a murderer," Rosie joked, giving me a shy smile as she fluttered her wings. "Until you turned up, we'd gone decades without a dead body, except by natural causes."

"Which this might still be," I said, the idea sounding even weaker the second time around.

"What? You think the world champion at hide and seek was in your spare room all this time?" Rosie pulled her mouth down at the corners before bursting into laughter. After a few seconds, she spluttered to a halt. "Sorry. I'm just in a state of shock."

"Do you think Esmerelda's behind it?"

Rosie's eyes opened wide and Posey rushed over to stand beside her sister. "Nobody here thinks that at all. The body must've been stashed in the walls all the time she lived there."

I remained silent, but inside I was calculating the likelihood of that scenario and coming up short. I'd found the body within a month of moving in, but the twins expected me to believe that my great aunt had somehow missed it for decades? No way.

Reggie and Darla made a move for the gate and I intercepted them midway. "You don't need to bring the tent," I assured them. "My parents can spend the night in my room, and I'll bunk on the couch."

"Sounds good but if I were you, I'd check with them before you make those plans too solid." Reggie lifted his dreads and repositioned them to one side. "Ben especially is keen on outdoor living."

"Or the idea of it, at least," Ben said, coming up behind me. "The reality might be different."

I sniggered, remembering a camping trip where my stepfather had set off believing he was Bear Grylls and returned as a diva. Even glamping couldn't forestall the horrors of a noisy forest at night.

"But you shouldn't have to take the sofa. I can do that."

"And leave me sharing a room with my mother?" I pulled a face. "No, thanks. And the two of you can't fit on our couch."

"What are you discussing?" Mum inserted herself into our group, grabbing my chin between her thumb and forefinger. "You look different."

"It's the clean air of a small town that does it," Syd

said, taking an enormous inhalation. "Makes your hair stand on end." He winked, then waved as a car pulled up to the curb. "There's Lucas. Since this case is"—he paused and tilted his head to one side while considering my mum and Ben—"standard issue."

"Nothing standard about it." My mother pulled me into a hug that cut off my ability to breathe. "The sooner you leave this horrid place, the better. First, you have a serial killer stalking the town and now you find a corpse inside your house."

"A long-dead one," I reminded her. "If there was any foul play involved, the perpetrator will probably be dead, too."

"As if that makes it any better." She pushed me out to arm's length and studied my face with the intensity only a loving parent can muster. "No. I want you back in Nelson."

"Especially with what's coming up," Ben said, earning a reproachful glance from my mother. "What? You haven't told her yet?"

"Told me what?" I disentangled myself and took a step back, checking Lucas and Syd were nearby in case I needed help. They were deep in conversation and I took a moment to enjoy the view before Ben grabbed my hand and brought me back to the conversation.

"Have you noticed your mother's sporting some new jewellery?"

My eyes flicked to her neck. Same locket.

Presumably with the same photos of her parents—my nonny and pop—inside. The same garnet and gold earrings dangled from her lobes as they always did unless she was going swimming whereupon they went straight into her wallet for safekeeping. The same bracelet encircled her wrist. 'The only present worth a damn that your father gave me,' as she liked to call it.

Then I saw the sparkling diamond on her finger.

"How beautiful," I said with a gasp, tipping my head closer to inspect the setting. "I love a princess cut. It looks just like an engagement ring."

I stared at my own hands for a second, trying to remember which hand the marital rings should go on before giving up. The best I could manage was to narrow it to two options.

My mother smiled so broadly that dimples appeared in either cheek. She extended her hand and cleared her throat. "It *is* an engagement ring."

"You're getting married?" My voice squeaked as a quick bit of mental arithmetic told me this ended a decade of the pair living in sin. "I mean, congratulations."

"That's not all." Ben rocked back on his feet, wriggling with excitement. "Tell her the best news."

"I think we should wait until we're settled." My mother glanced around the yard, frowning at the throng of people still gathered. "This wasn't how I pictured it."

"Pictured what?" Ben's enthusiasm had transmitted itself to me and I grabbed hold of her hand. "Tell me."

"We're pregnant!" The news shot out of Ben's mouth like a grenade exploding. "You're going to have a little brother or sister."

CHAPTER FOUR

*M*y shock at the news took a full hour to dissipate. Until then, my brain didn't know what my mouth was saying. It presumably offered many varied forms of congratulations. Certainly, there was a lot of hugging going on.

Luckily, Rosie and Posey heard a rumour on the town grapevine that the police were nosing around my house. They turned up, took one look at the situation, and declared there was no way Mum and Ben were staying in the murder house with a baby on the way.

I had vague memories of expressing a desire for a brother or sister when I was much smaller. Almost everyone at school possessed a sibling and the thought of another tiny human in the house seemed fun.

However, my mother had shaken her head at the notion, insisting one was enough.

Now, just as I reached an age where having a baby had started to be a consideration for me rather than a dreaded fear, she'd obviously changed her mind.

"Don't worry," Ben insisted as my mind finally cleared. "There's no way a baby will displace your position in the family."

"You'll always be my number one daughter," Mum agreed cheerfully, patting her flat belly. "Get prepared to boss this one around."

I hadn't been worried about that aspect at all. Not until the reassurances came flooding in.

Rosie installed my parents in a sleepout at the back of their property. The addition contained a comfortable four rooms—bigger than the flat I'd vacated a few weeks before.

"Don't worry about a thing," Posey insisted as my mother tried to offer payment. "This is just going to waste, otherwise. It'll be nice to know someone's making good use of this space."

"You can sleep on the couch here," my mother said, reaching over to squeeze my hand.

"I'm fine at home." There were so many new things to process, I had to have some space.

"But…" Mum's face crumpled into a concerned expression. "The skeleton," she mouthed.

"Is too dead to hurt me?"

"You can't be too careful," Ben insisted as he opened every drawer and cabinet, investigating the lodgings as if it were the crime scene. "Besides, the twins have offered to make us a full English breakfast, just like staying at a BNB. We don't want you to miss out."

Judging from the shade of green on my mother's face, she hadn't made it past the joys of morning sickness.

"Why did you bring your kitten along?" My mum collapsed onto the king-sized bed as though she'd just disembarked from a twelve-hour flight. "She can't be comfortable stuffed down the front of your jacket."

"I didn't want the police tripping over her or accidentally locking her inside something."

"How have you even found time to adopt a kitten? You've only been here a few weeks."

As I thought of everything I'd gone through in that short space of time, picking up a kitten faded in comparison. But I couldn't tell my mother any of that! "She came with the house. Muffin was Great Aunt Esmerelda's kitten."

A trio of light sneezes greeted that news. "Well, I'm allergic to her. How about you leave us alone to settle in and we'll call to make plans for dinner later?"

The making plans part sounded good. I wish my mother had thought to call me with plans before they'd turned up on my doorstep.

"Sure." I took a step towards the exit, then squeezed my eyes shut. Although I'd avoided the subject in every phone call home, I wanted to ask my mother about the whole inheritance malarkey. Especially the bit about not receiving notification until it was almost too late.

"Stop squeezing me." Muffin struggled in my arms.

"Whoops." Ben scooped her up as she jumped free and made a beeline for the door. "Looks like you've got a little escape artist here."

"Sorry." I let Muffin sit on my shoulder, out of harm's way.

"What was all that about?" she demanded as I took the cowards way out and left, waving goodbye to Rosie and Posey. "I thought I was done for."

"When I get nervous, my muscles tense up."

"What do you have to be nervous about here?" Muffin glanced back at the lovely rose runner threading through the entrance arch. "It's far more welcoming than a skeleton stashed in an upstairs cupboard."

"I want to ask them why nobody ever talked about Esmerelda or being a pixie."

"Oh, that." Muffin scooted from one shoulder to the other, before settling her butt into the crook of my neck. "Considering they'd never heard of Brody either, it makes them sound like they're not even related."

"Except…" I waved at my hair and pointy features. "We are."

"Write down what you want to know," Muffin said with a yawn, as though she hadn't just woken from a nap after a long night's sleep. "If you have your thoughts in order, it'll make it much easier to quiz them."

"Perhaps." It sounded like a good idea, but I wondered how much concentration I could muster with the police running through my home and a dead body upstairs. "Do you know who the skeleton belongs to?"

The only reply were the long breaths of a snoozing cat. Hm.

Heading home was the last thing I wanted to do, so I walked in the direction of the library. The talk this morning might have been idle conjecture but a job in such a quiet place sounded divine. Besides, they might even have some old town history in their stacks that could help with the current problem.

"No pets," the librarian whispered as I approached the front desk. She did a double-take through her thick horn-rimmed glasses as Muffin woke up, stretching. "Wait. Is that Esme's familiar?"

"Mine, now." I held out my hand and received a limp-wristed shake. "I'm Elisa Hamilton. Esmerelda's great-niece."

"Great-niece or a great niece?" Muffin asked in a

small voice as she rearranged herself, using my hair as a pulley system. "Hey, Patsy. How're things?"

Patsy pulled up part of the counter and slipped through. "They'll be terrible if I don't get you two out of sight. It doesn't do to set a precedent. Follow me."

She led us between two high shelves stacked with books and unlocked a side room with an old-fashioned key. The door protested as she shoved it open, the wood squeaking loudly against the frame.

Inside, a table was covered with old books in various states of disrepair. The air was at least five degrees cooler than the main library—enough so I felt grateful for Muffin's warmth.

"Touch nothing!" Patsy said, one forefinger raised in warning. "These books contain more knowledge than half of the town."

"Which half?" Muffin asked, using my body as a ladder to reach the floor. "Because if it's the supernatural side, then I'm insulted."

"Of course, I didn't mean you, deary." Patsy put the large key in her pocket before primping her hair. "Now, who sent you?"

"Nobody sent us." I stared at my kitten in confusion, but her face held the same nonplussed expression as mine. "I heard there might be an opening for a volunteer librarian."

"Did you now?" Patsy pressed her lips together and

stuck her face uncomfortably close to mine. "And who told you that?"

I pointed to Muffin, my words drying up under the librarian's intense scrutiny. Her silver hair caught the light from the high window and turned the tight curls into a helmet, ready for battle.

"And?" Patsy arched an eyebrow, staring at my familiar until I crouched to let her run into the safety of my arms.

"We don't know what you're talking about," I spluttered. "My roommate went for a job interview this morning and we got to talking about possible openings and this place came up."

I suffered under Patsy's rigorous gaze for another minute, then the woman relented—sitting at the table and waving me into a chair. "That's okay, then. There've just been a few odd things happening around here this morning and it pays to be sure."

Still completely baffled, I silently nodded. The skeleton at home suddenly seemed more attractive than being seated here.

"Does that mean there isn't a volunteer role open?" Muffin asked, blinking up at me. "Only, it'd be good to get this one out of the house during the day."

"So you can nap undisturbed?" Patsy gave her an understanding wink. "We're always in the market for help, as long as you understand the role will be unpaid."

I was about to decline the generous offer—another volunteer role far away from this strange librarian would be preferable—when I heard a loud snort from the main room. The floorboards underneath my chair creaked as something gigantic shifted its weight outside.

"Um, do you...?" Patsy trailed off as another snort echoed around the library, this time sounding as though it came from inside our room. She cleared her throat. "Do you hear that?"

Muffin tapped a paw on my hand. "Get some dust ready."

With a shaking hand, I scraped a few loose flakes into my palm and sat, trembling. The jump as the next snort came a mere foot away from my ear must have been enough proof for Patsy.

"Begone monster!" she shouted, standing and waving her arms. "We have pixie power on our side now."

I closed my eyes, wishing I had the same belief in my abilities that Patsy did. Pages on the volume nearest to me ruffled in a warm breeze—the invisible monster's breath.

"If you don't show yourself, I'll use my powers to reveal you to the room." I held the dust to my lips, a scratch card in my mind with the silver paint peeling back. "Whatever trouble you're up to, you can perform it in plain sight."

"Who cares about seeing it or not?" Patsy jumped across the table and took hold of my hand. "Whatever this invisible creature is, I don't want it hanging around my library. How'd you like a dose of poison to breathe in, monster?"

She squeezed her eyes shut and blew the dust from my palm. It fell on the floor, turning from all the colours of the rainbow to a dull grey as it did so.

"Get more," Patsy yelled, pushing my hand away with disgust. "This thing's been tormenting me for an hour, trying to get into the archives and steal all of Oakleaf Glade's secrets."

"If the universe says no to my magic, there's nothing more I can do."

"It's not the universe turning you down, lovey. You just don't know how to use the powers you've got. Give me some." Patsy held out her hand, clicking her fingers. "I'll show this creature who's the real monster in town."

With one last snort, whatever presence had been in the room departed, fluttering loose pages in its wake.

"And stay gone," Patsy yelled after it before turning the key in the lock, trapping us inside the small room. "Now. How about we discuss training you up to do battle in return for some spare pixie dust?"

CHAPTER FIVE

"These are the volumes with the most relevant information," Patsy said from atop a ladder, reaching for the books on the highest shelf. "We keep them up here so no one can happen upon them by accident."

"What's wrong with people reading them?" I asked, astonished that the town librarian seemed so intent on keeping people from books.

"Knowledge can be a weapon in the wrong hands," she intoned with grave solemnity before jumping to the floor. "And we only want it to be a weapon for good."

"What will this teach me?" I asked, eager for any shortcut. The thickness of the books combined with the teeny tiny writing on the page made me think there weren't enough hours in a day.

"Loopholes," Patsy said, dusting her hands together. "All the universal laws in practice in the world can always be got around if you have the right mindset and good intentions."

"Is this the stuff your library monster was after?" Muffin said, sniffing at the book and wrinkling her nose at the dusty smell. "Seems dangerous."

"Only if the people on the wrong side of the battle get hold of them."

"Battle?" I stared at Patsy in mounting horror. "Is there a war on?"

She planted her hands on her ample hips and pursed her lips. "There's always a war on. Haven't you heard of good versus evil? Did you think it had died out just because everyone nowadays is glued to their screens?"

"Considering you tried to use pixie dust to kill something before we could find out its intentions, good and evil seem to be relative positions."

Patsy sniffed and turned on her heel, marching back to the front desk. "That's the talk that loses wars."

"If my familiar doesn't want me reading these books," I said, following along with trepidation, "then I don't think I should. Muffin's got way more experience with pixiedom than I do."

"And far less than my family." Patsy opened the book to the last page and pulled out a card, tapping on the last name. "See here? That's your great aunt. If she

41

didn't have a problem reading these books, I don't see why you should."

The name scrawled on the card could have been anyone. My generation wasn't into the habit of deciphering cursive and the smudged black pen didn't make the job any easier. Still, judging from Muffin's expression, Patsy wasn't lying.

"Read them and if you don't want to use the information, don't." Patsy shrugged. "It's up to you. All I'm saying is that if an invisible creature tries to get hold of the most sacred documents in town, it might come in handy to know what's in them."

"Is there anything in here that would help us identify a skeleton?"

"Would that be a pixie stored in someone's upstairs cupboard?"

My mouth fell open as I stared at Patsy. "How did you hear about that already? It only happened a few hours ago."

The librarian tapped the side of her nose and appeared as pleased as punch. "I keep my ear to the ground. Nothing's a secret in a town as small as Oakleaf Glade." She wrinkled her nose. "Especially when some supernaturals can read minds."

"You can read minds?" My mouth dropped open, and I wanted to pinch myself. No matter how strange the supernatural world appeared, every day brought a new bunch of weirdness.

"I can't but many in town can. Considering I'm the town librarian, I'd rather everybody got their information from books, but what can you do?"

"What type of supernatural is Patsy, then?" I whispered to Muffin as I staggered from the building, weighed down with the heaviest books I'd carried since high school tried to rearrange my spine in a permanent curve. "She doesn't have wings."

"A book goblin. She hoards novels the same way a jeweller goblin hoards gold."

"I need one of those charts like they have in the fish and chip shops, with all the fish varieties laid out."

Muffin gave me a puzzled glance. "You don't even like fish."

"No! For supernaturals. Is there anything like that available?"

"Yeah. It's called a town meeting. Held on the first Monday of each quarter. Everyone has to wear a name and species badge."

"Really?" My eyes glowed until I saw Muffin sniggering under her breath. "Don't be mean. And why do you keep avoiding my question about who the skeleton belongs to?"

She arched her back and snuffled at the inside of my jacket. "I don't know what you mean."

"Every time I ask, you pretend to be asleep."

It took me a few moments to realise the kitten was at it again. She gave a small whine as something crossed her path in the dream world, then her breath evened into the slow exhalations of sleep.

"Boo!" I yelled to startle her awake.

"Boo yourself," Maisie said, appearing out of nowhere as usual. "Who're you trying to frighten?"

"My familiar isn't being very helpful today."

Maisie leaned closer, examining the kitten in detail before pulling back. "She looks normal to me. Why are you carrying half the town library? Isn't there a law against checking out too many books?"

"If there's not, there should be." I adjusted my grip on the book bag while trying not to squash Muffin. "Patsy made me take them all for research."

"Good job." Maisie floated close to read the titles, then arched an eyebrow. "Aren't you already a pixie? Why are you reading about them?"

"Loopholes," I said in my most mysterious voice. "Apparently, lawyers aren't the only ones who need to know legal ways around things."

"Ugh. Legalise bores me stupid." Maisie drifted towards a shop window, surveying a hundred ice cream flavours she'd never get to taste. "I heard you found a guest who forgot to check out."

I rolled my eyes. The real magic would be keeping anything secret in this town. "Any idea on who the skeleton belongs to?"

"Not a clue."

"Can't you ask your otherworldly friends?"

Maisie stared at me with narrowed eyes. "I can't tell if you're being facetious or not, so I'll just settle for saying I have no more contact with the other side than you do."

"But you're…" I waved at her insubstantial form.

"Here, is the word you're searching for. If you want to cross into another realm to search for the person stored upstairs in your house, go for it. I'm happy right where I am."

"Can I do that?"

The ghost burst into laughter. "If you run into traffic, maybe. Do you have a death wish coming on?" Once her amusement subsided, Maisie tilted her head to one side. "You could always start at the memorial gardens. Send a cloud of pixie magic out to find the skeleton's grave."

Now it was my turn to laugh. "Sure. Except the thing that would usually be stored in the plot is on its way to police headquarters."

"People often set aside spaces for their loved ones whether or not they have a body to bury. Unless the poor dead person didn't have any friends or family, they'll probably have something there. A plaque at the very least."

After a detour home to drop off my back-breaking load of books, we hastened to the Oakleaf Glade memorial gardens. A high wrought-iron gate twisted into a repeating figure-eight design was pushed back, welcoming us inside. A sign warned that the gardens were open from eight to eight only and trespassers would be prosecuted.

"As though anyone would hang around a graveyard at night," I said with a shudder. Even in the warm light of midday, some of the older stones and plaques made me feel uneasy. The children's garden just about broke my heart with its whirling toys made in bright reds, yellows, and greens. I averted my eyes as we walked past.

"This is the oldest part," Maisie said in a strange voice as we entered the centre of the gardens. "The entire history of Oakleaf Glade's founding fathers can be found in this section."

I read some older plaques, noticing familiar names popping up again and again. Spicer. Hunter. Berwick. Matthews.

"Oh, this is your grave," I exclaimed, bending in close to read the faded stone. "What a pretty inscription." When I glanced at her, Maisie held her hands over her eyes. "Don't you want to see?"

"No, thanks. Keep moving. Or, better yet, put your magic to use so we can find out if the skeleton in your house is attached to a name in this garden."

"Be careful," Muffin said in a low voice before bouncing off in chase of a butterfly. Her kitten wiles weren't equal to the powers of flight and she soon returned to my side.

"What am I being careful of?" I paused with a coating of dust in my palm, a shiver playing music up and down my spine.

"The dead have greater powers than most people give them credit for. You know I can't see ghosts so I can't save you from a malevolent one if it comes forth from a grave."

"Maisie'll get them, won't you?"

But the ghost had disappeared, perhaps freaked out by her own grave.

"I'll be careful." With a soft breath, I blew a cloud of bright violet across the gardens. It floated in the breeze, playing a game with the leaves of a nearby tree before settling inside a gated section. I followed along at a sedate pace, checking in all directions for some imaginary foe.

"These are the Spicer family plots," Muffin said in a sad voice, her eyes welling with tears. "The freshest one is Esmerelda."

I picked up the kitten and held her close, picking my way through the gate and into the reserved space with care.

The cloud was fading but there was still enough of the vibrant colour to highlight the plaque affixed at the head of the grave.

"Esmerelda Jane Spicer," I read out from the stone. "Forever Pixie."

"Your magic must've got it wrong," Muffin said

with a sniff. "Perhaps you should study those books and try again. What were you focusing on?"

I shook my head, happy to take the blame for the pixie dust's failure. "Unless Esmerelda wasn't really who she claimed to be," I said, trying for a lame joke and succeeding.

Muffin scowled and bounced away, chasing a field mouse through the long grass at the boundary edge. I knelt beside the stone and traced the carved edges with my fingertips. "And if you weren't you, who were you?" I whispered, the idea taking hold in my mind.

"NEEDLESS TO SAY," Lucas said with no sign of irony, "if you come across anything inside the house you think might be related to this... um... discovery, please let us know." He tucked his notebook away, smiling so his laugh lines creased his face. "Although, I hope for your sake, there isn't."

"For my sake?"

He shrugged and turned to gaze at the street. "You've already landed in the middle of a few rough patches and you only turned up in Oakleaf Glade a minute ago. If these weird things keep happening, it won't give you a chance to get to know our good side."

Lucas appeared so earnest I couldn't help but return his smile. "Well, I'll keep my fingers crossed."

He explained that he and Syd had contacted members of my family to press for more information about the discovery. A team had also used echolocation equipment to scan the old building for any further anomalies. "They found no more bones inside but nothing's ever one hundred percent guaranteed unless you knock the place down."

That might be too much of a strain even for a self-repairing house. "I'll take my chances, thanks." In the back of my mind, I also thought a call to Reggie to have him sniff the entire home over could be in order.

"Judging from the age of the remains, you shouldn't have any worries even if the death came about from violent means," he hastened to assure me. "I'll leave the precise dating to the experts but if someone turns up on your doorstep with a walker... Maybe think twice before letting them in."

Muffin didn't appear nearly as amused as I was. She hissed at Lucas until he waved goodbye and walked out the gate.

"There's no need to be rude," I said, keeping the door open a slit as I watched Lucas bend over to pick up a piece of litter from the footpath. I must remember to plant something in future to encourage a repeat performance. "PC Bronson is just watching out for our welfare."

"If he remembers who you are for long enough."

"Wow. Someone got out of the wrong side of the bed this morning."

"Yeah. The side where your family shows up out of the blue and people besmirch my old mistress."

I fetched the biscuit tin from the pantry and pulled the grouchy kitten into my lap. "Nobody is pointing fingers at Esmerelda," I said as I fed her a peach custard muffin. "It's too early to know what went on."

"Your magic pointed the finger."

"And we both know how inexperienced I am at that."

"I'm going to poke about upstairs and see what damage the police have done. Then I really need a nap."

I refrained from rolling my eyes until the kitten had left the room. If I worked on Muffin's timetable, I'd be asleep for twenty hours a day.

Keeping one ear out for her movements in the spare room, I booted up the laptop and typed in a search query for Esmerelda. It proved to be a more popular name than I would have given credit for—so much so I had to narrow the search using her elder sister Dimity's name.

A reference to an old paper sat near the top of the results. It linked to a tragic scan of the original newspaper, crumpled and yellowed from sunlight. The birth notice was a third of the way down the page. Happy tidings from a bygone era.

Dimity Spicer. Esmerelda Spicer. Rose Spicer.

Not twins. Triplets.

Knowing Dimity was older than Esmerelda by seventeen minutes, I had a reasonable guess at where Rose sat in the birth order. The youngest. The youngest daughter of a youngest daughter.

Rose should have been a pixie.

CHAPTER SIX

"In theory, if a pixie died and therefore qualified a sibling for the role, the older sister could take over the mantel," Rosie said with a thoughtful stare. "But that's only in theory. I've never heard of such a thing happening in practice."

"And you don't know for sure how those three came out." Posey's usually smiling face was clouded over with a worried frown. "Just because the paper printed their name that way, doesn't mean that's the order their mum popped them out."

"But it explains everything, doesn't it?" As I scanned the twins' faces, I saw the connections I'd made weren't reciprocated. "If Esmerelda stored her younger sister's body in the—"

"Woah!" The twins lifted their hands in unison.

Posey opened her mouth but closed it without speaking.

"You didn't know your great aunt, so we'll overlook the appalling accusation you just made." Rosie's lips twisted and she shook her head. "Esmerelda was the sweetest thing. She only ever used her magic to help others and benefit the community."

"Sure. But a body was in the wall and Syd said it belonged to a pixie."

"Just stop." Posey's eyes filled with tears and her voice sounded strangled. "I know there's been bad blood in your family, but this attack is completely unwarranted. Perhaps when you welcome your new baby brother or sister into the world, you'll get an idea of how impossible what you're saying is."

"I don't mean she killed her or anything."

"That's enough!" Rosie's cheeks were flushing crimson. "We don't know who the body belongs to or even if Esmerelda knew it was there. Until we're in possession of those facts, rampant conjecture will only lead to harm."

"Sorry." My face flooded with hot blood as I realised how I must have sounded. "I'm creeped out knowing a pixie was trapped in the walls of my house. It's hard to make a home with the bones of your ancestors trapped in an upstairs cupboard."

Posey wrung her hands. "Everything about it is

awful. We should turn our minds to happier subjects such as your mum getting married and having a baby."

"Did somebody mention my name?" Ben called from the doorway. "If anyone is volunteering to be a wedding planner, I'll take you up on the offer."

"Come on in," Posey said, beaming. "Both of us have been planning our dream weddings since we were little girls, so we have a ton of ideas between us."

"Although," Rosie said in a warning voice, "we can't use up all our great ideas. There's still a chance one or both of us might need them ourselves."

Posey cackled with laughter. "When's the last time you went on a date? The nineties?"

"I've still got some moves." Rosie spun around the room in a one-sided tango. "Any man would be lucky to have me."

"Any man would be lucky to have either of you," I said, backing towards the door as I caught Ben's eye. "Tell Mum I'll drop by to see her later."

"Take your time. She's still trying to decide on a restaurant for dinner."

Out of the three establishments open in town. Poor man. My mother could make a spur-of-the-moment decision about anything except food. Even when she narrowed down her dining options, the entire table would be on pause while she picked something from the menu.

From the twins' house, I quickly walked to the Births, Deaths, and Marriages office. Instead of making vague accusations to the fairies, I should have started there. "I need three birth certificates," I informed the uninterested assistant behind the counter. "For my great aunts."

"Names and dates of birth?"

I read them off the screen on my phone and waited while the woman tapped the information into her computer. "They've not been born long enough," she said after a moment's scrutiny. "Come back when they reach one hundred years."

"Excuse me?"

The receptionist opened a drawer and pulled out a pamphlet. "See here? You can only order another person's birth certificate if it was issued a hundred years ago or longer."

"But it's for family."

She rolled her eyes. "Everything's for family, these days. The number of people I have through here, researching their deceased whanau as though it's the secret to a happy life. Just let things be, that's what I say. No need to drag all that old stuff up when there's today to be lived."

"Right." I opened the pamphlet and pretended to read the pages while my mind worked through the problem. If only I'd brought Muffin along with me, she could have stolen the addresses to access the information like she'd done the last time I needed something.

On the other hand, hearing her old mistress being accused of sororicide probably wouldn't be on her list of favourite things to do.

"I understand your rules but is there any way you can help to settle an old family argument?"

"Probably not." The receptionist picked up a pencil and doodled a box on her calendar pad, then sighed and asked, "What do you want, then?"

"My great aunts were triplets. My uncle insists Dimity is the oldest and Esmerelda is the youngest, but my mother says that Rose is the one who was born last."

The woman's bland face stared at me. "And this is something that keeps you up nights, is it?"

"It would just be nice to settle it once and for all." I leaned over the counter and lowered my voice to a whisper, though there was nobody else in the room. "Especially, if I'm right."

She gave another sigh but tapped on her computer. "Okay. Usually, a birth certificate doesn't register the time, just the date, but in the cases of multiple births it's standard."

"Oh, good. Why?"

The receptionist wrinkled her nose. "Birth order used to matter a lot more than it does now. Back in the day, entire estates would be left solely to the eldest, and you didn't want to waste money determining who that was."

"And am I right?"

The woman leaned forward to glean the information, then beamed. "One of you is right but, as I already stated, I'm not allowed to pass that information to you. Not until the birth has been registered over one hundred years."

And that was the last answer I was going to get.

I DROPPED into the local bakery, bringing a smile to the server's face. "The usual?"

The usual was half a dozen muffins and had already been served to me once that day. Given the lady behind the counter was human, I didn't want to know what she thought I got up to with so many baked treats.

I patted my belly, realising I disposed of my fair share of the muffins. Especially, when they came with hokey pokey crumbled over the top.

The curve of my abdomen reminded me of my mother, and how she'd soon be swelling out until she couldn't see her toes. "Do you have any gingerbread men or something like that?"

"Sure. How many?"

I got a dozen just to be safe. When I'd been sick

with vertigo a few years back, nibbling on gingerbread men had been the only way to eat while staving off the accompanying nausea. Hopefully, my mother's metabolism embraced the same spices.

Since I was already there, I also picked up a few fairy cupcakes for my favourite fairies. Although I doubted the bakery came close to the fresh baking prowess of the twins, it was the thought that counted.

Just before I returned to Rosie and Posey's house, I steeled my spine, ready to ask my mother some difficult questions. Unfortunately, the steel had somehow performed a feat of alchemy and transformed into jelly by the time I visited her in the sleepout. The image of her lying on her back while Ben rubbed her feet wasn't conducive to hardnosed questioning.

"Tavern Café," I told her when she complained there were too many choices for dinner, and it was giving her a headache. "Brody works there and the food's delicious."

"Ah, yes. Your mysterious cousin Brody, who I've never heard of."

"Hardly mysterious." I checked my watch and grimaced. "And you'd probably have met him by now if we hadn't made our gruesome discovery."

In fact, even if his job interview had run over, he should be home, finding out all about the morning's events from someone other than me.

"I'll make a reservation and come by again to pick you up at five-thirty."

My mother cocked an eyebrow. "Does your car still go?"

"The restaurant is within walking distance but yes, if we need it my car is fully operational."

"Good, because ours sounds like it's on its last legs." Mum batted Ben on the shoulder. "You should call up a mechanic in case we need to leave town in a hurry."

"Brody can probably help you out for free," I said, remembering how he'd fixed my old Nissan Pulsar when I first arrived in town. "And you can quiz him on his family history while he's doing it."

The segue, *speaking of family history*, was all set up to go but when I opened my mouth, Maisie appeared in the back yard. Thank goodness she had the decency to just wave instead of frightening the life out of me.

"Gotta go." I leaned over and planted a big kiss on my mother's cheek. "Be ready at five."

"You're not coming until five-thirty," she said with a grin, rearranging herself on the bed.

"And I know you. If you aim to get ready then, we'll be waiting to leave here until seven." I turned to Ben and winked. "You should remember to tell your new wedding planners about Mum's tendency for lateness."

"Here comes the bride. Eventually."

I left as Mum aimed a friendly kick at Ben's side. "What's going on?" I asked Maisie as she floated above me with a worried expression. "Have you found out something about the skeleton?"

"No, but you should get home. A strange man is stomping around the house, yelling for the owner to come out."

I pulled a face. "Doesn't sound like the type of thing I'd like to get home for."

"The last words I heard were, 'If you don't come outside, I'll get an axe and chop my way in!'"

After a shocked second to digest the news, I began to run.

CHAPTER SEVEN

*L*ucas pulled up outside just as I reached home, winded and unable to explain any more than I'd done over the phone.

Luckily—or unluckily, since I aimed to live a peaceful life—a man's voice was shouting from behind the house. With a gesture to warn me off following him, Lucas drew a baton and stalked along the side of the property, pressing close against the wall.

"Get out here," the man shouted. "Either you show yourself or I'll break the door down and drag you outside."

"What on earth does he think I've done to him?" I whispered to Maisie, equal parts afraid and baffled. Sure, there'd been a few sketchy incidents since I'd arrived in town, but I thought they were all done and dusted.

"If you think you're dragging my sister into whatever mess you've got yourself into, you've got another think coming!"

A cold chill settled on my scalp, running along my shoulders and numbing my arms. I recognised that voice. Or, at least, I thought I did. It was hard to tell since I'd never heard him screaming at the top of his lungs before.

"Uh, PC Bronson?" I waved to him from the gate and, when he didn't turn, realised I was still speaking in a whisper. "Lucas!"

He jumped, startled, and I gestured for him to come back to me. In turn, Lucas waved me away, tightening the grip on the baton.

"Uncle Pete," I yelled at the top of my lungs, scared an altercation was about to take place that would wind up with both men coming to harm. "This is Elisa. Stop yelling at the house and come around the front if you want to talk to me."

Lucas made a hushing gesture, but that ship had sailed.

"And behave yourself when you do," I added. "Because the police are here and they're capable of tackling you to the ground if you try anything foolish."

My red-faced uncle poked his head around the corner, giving a sniff when he saw me. "Elisa. I thought you had more brains than to come to this place and take over this disastrous legacy."

"Nice to see you, too, Uncle Pete." I folded my arms across my chest as he sauntered closer as though he hadn't just shouted loud enough for the neighbourhood to hear. "Want to tell me what this is about?"

"I got a call from the police telling me there's a murder victim stashed in my aunt's house. Just as I told them it was nothing to do with our side of the family, they informed me it very much was." He came to a stop two metres distant and scanned me from head to toe with an air of disappointment. "I thought Kayla raised you better."

"Better than what? Better than someone who tried to cheat me out of my inheritance?"

Uncle Pete gave a derisive laugh. "Inheritance? Is that what you're calling it? Curse would be a better word." He tugged at the back of his hair, staring at mine as he did so. "I see you went through with the whole thing."

Lucas stepped between the two of us, planting his back to Uncle Pete and talking to me in a soft voice. "Are you okay? I can still haul him down to the station."

"On what charges?" My uncle sneered. "Being concerned for my niece's welfare?"

"Around here, we call that disturbing the peace," Lucas said, his gaze never wavering from mine.

"We're fine." I scratched my fingers across my scalp

just in case, though the resulting trail of glittering pixie dust seemed fainter than usual. "It's just a family dispute."

"They're the ones most likely to end badly."

"If anything happens, I've got the police station number on speed dial."

"Ain't that the truth." Lucas sighed and stepped away. "It's a rare day when we don't get a callout on behalf of Miss Elisa Hamilton."

"Ms, thank you very much."

"If you lay a finger on her—" Lucas pointed straight between Uncle Pete's eyes.

My uncle held his hands up. "Nobody will hurt anyone. We're just going to have a chat."

"Do it at a lower volume, will you? The neighbour's curtains are already twitching."

As I turned to watch Lucas leave, I saw he was right. Across the road, a woman stood close enough to her net curtains for me to recognise her shape and a few houses along, an elderly man was collecting his mail at snail speed.

"Come on inside," I said with some reluctance. It felt odd to invite him into the home he'd deliberately tried to prevent me inheriting. But my pride wasn't about to give the neighbours any more of a show than they'd already received. "I could do with a cup of coffee."

As I stepped inside, it took my mind a while to work out what it was seeing. Scraps of paper floated in the air, some burning. One drifted close to the smoke alarm, setting off its piercing cry.

"Grab a towel," I shouted at my uncle, covering my ears as the sound made my head ring. How was anybody meant to escape a fire with that terrifying noise scattering their thoughts? When he tossed me a tea towel, I grabbed a chair and waved the cloth near the device.

Blessed silence returned in a few seconds, giving me the space to look around again. The stack of library books I'd dumped on the table earlier was now in tiny pieces. They looked like a pile of sticks after having a run-in with a wood-chipping machine.

"What's all this?" Uncle Pete asked in dismay just as I was about to accuse him of having broken in and wreaked havoc. "Have the witches got you involved in occult rituals already?"

"What witches?" I shook my hands, flapping away his concerns. "This isn't down to *me*. Someone's obviously…" I trailed off as I heard a faint mewing from the lounge. "Muffin!"

She crawled out from behind a cushion on the sofa, trembling from head to toe. "Where have you been? The world's turned upside down."

I broke off half a muffin top from the fresh batch

and tempted her fully out of hiding. "Do you know who did this?"

"Him." Muffin stared at my uncle with her back arched and her hairs standing on end. "He was shouting out threats when the books began self-destructing. It must have been a curse."

"Or a complete coincidence." Uncle Pete rapped his knuckles on the table. "You saw me outside. I just wanted somebody to come to the door to talk."

"Yeah, I did see you. It's hardly the display to set my mind at rest." I plucked a torn page from the air as it floated past and frowned. "But unless you've got magic at your disposal…"

"Magic. I wouldn't touch the evil stuff with a barge pole." He rubbed his forehead, making the wrinkles appear even deeper. "Neither should you if you know what's good for you."

"It's not evil. The universe won't let it be used that way."

He rubbed a finger over his eyebrow, smoothing the hairs. "That's not my experience."

I coaxed Muffin into the kitchen with the rest of the treats and patted her as much as she'd allow. "You didn't see anyone?"

She shook her head and settled back on her hind legs, leaving the bulk of the muffin untouched. "Just the shouting outside and the library books tearing themselves apart."

"This situation is exactly the kind of thing I wanted to protect you from," Uncle Pete said, talking over the kitten. "What are these books, anyway?" He picked up some torn pieces and tried to fit them together.

"Nothing to do with you." I snatched them out of his hand. "They're just old books from the library that have left me with a lot of explaining to do."

"You should leave town immediately." Pete helped himself to a chair and drummed his fingers on the table. "Once you become a target in Oakleaf Glade, it doesn't stop." He shuddered. "The things I saw here as a boy, you wouldn't believe, but they've been haunting my nightmares ever since. If you ever want to find peace again, get out while you still can."

"While I still can? What does that even mean?" I gestured at the front door. "If I want to go back to scraping a living from day to day and never knowing if I'll ever get another full-time job, I can walk straight out the front door."

"You don't understand the hold this place gets on you." Uncle Pete buried his face into his hands and for a moment I thought he was crying. Then he raised his head again, his eyes dry. "The closer I got to the town welcome sign, the more I could feel it pulling at me." He thumped his chest with a fist. "Right in here."

"Nonsense." Muffin ran up my arm to perch on my shoulder. "There's nothing holding anyone here except the same things that hold anybody to a community where they feel cherished and loved."

"If you don't believe me," Uncle Pete said, staring straight into my eyes. "Then try it. Do you really want to stay in this place given what the police have just found?" He grasped hold of my hand. "Come and visit with my family for a while. You know all your cousins will love the chance to catch up with you."

"Mum's here. I can hardly skip town when she's come down to see me."

"Kayla and Ben are welcome to come. There's enough room now most of the kids have moved out. What do you say?"

His grip on my hand had grown increasingly tight, and I pulled it free. "I say, the police told me to stay in town in case I need to answer any more questions."

At that, Uncle Pete rolled his eyes. "They can hardly think you had something to do with a decades-old body hidden upstairs. You have a phone, don't you?" At my nod, he continued, "Well, then. You're not fleeing the scene, you're just finding somewhere more pleasant to stay."

Putting aside my distrust, I felt a pang of longing for the hours I'd spent at Uncle Pete's during my childhood. As an only child, my home had always been quiet unless I had friends over. A half-dozen cousins tumbling in and out of the house meant my uncle and aunt's house had been anything but.

"You're not going to leave, are you?" Muffin jumped onto the table to place a paw on my hand and stare into my face. "Once we leave town, your pixie powers will diminish. You probably won't be able to hear me, and you won't be able to cast a pixie spell."

A new fact that I didn't know quite what to do with.

"If you're not going to come home with me, then I'll have to find a place in town," Uncle Pete said with a sigh. "I don't suppose you know anywhere cheap."

"You're staying?" I pulled my mouth down at the corners. "What happened to this place being hell on earth?"

"Since it's the place my niece and sister are staying, and they're both in trouble, I hardly have a choice." He stood up, then leaned over to pat my shoulder. "But the offer is still open if you change your mind."

"Not likely," Muffin said, rearing onto her hind legs.

"Cute kittie," Uncle Pete said, tickling her under the chin.

"Burn in the fires of hell, demon."

His smile wavered and a missing puzzle piece slotted into place. I snapped my fingers. "You can hear Muffin."

Uncle Pete's face went still. "I don't know what you're talking about."

"Before. She said you were cursed, and you denied it, saying the whole thing was coincidental."

He tilted his head to one side, eyes narrowing. "I was responding to you." But the game was up, and his face said he knew it. With a huff, he sat back in the chair. "Fine. Yes, I can hear your familiar. I'm as much of a pixie as you, though being male it doesn't count for very much."

CHAPTER EIGHT

"We used to visit here all the time, growing up," Uncle Pete said, holding a cold beer in his hand.

I'd pulled one from the fridge in the hope it would loosen his tongue and my ploy worked. Either that, or he desperately wanted to share the memories with someone.

"It must've been great as a kid." The expansive attic rooms and the large back yard seemed custom made for entertaining children, even on rainy days. Not to mention clomping up and down the steep stairs until an adult screamed for them to stop.

"It was fine until I hit puberty and understood more about what goes on in this town. The supernaturals might appear harmless at first, but there's a reason they're all gathered here, in one weird and creepy spot."

"Oakleaf Glade isn't creepy." I took a sip from my drink, a sugar-free cola I kept buying to make up for the enormous quantities of sugar I was ingesting daily in the form of Muffin's favourite food. "Even the memorial gardens are lovely."

"Wait until it hits the depths of winter. Not so lovely then."

I stood up to grab another can from the fridge. "Being colder doesn't make it weird. Seasons are normal, in case you hadn't noticed."

"They have ghosts here, did you know?"

Maisie, who had just drifted into the lounge to see how her warning turned out, seemed flattered to be mentioned. She winked at me as she floated closer.

"Horrible things," Uncle Pete said while Maisie recoiled. "They wake you at night to tell you all their problems. I started to see them when I was fourteen. I mean, what could I do?"

"Apparently, if you ask them what they want, they go away," I said, fighting to keep my voice steady as Maisie's expression exploded in a fit of apoplexy. "The one I've met has been charming and helpful."

Her ego assuaged, Maisie flounced from the room, presumably seeking somewhere safer to lurk.

"The ones who used to visit me would tell me horrible

stories. Some were murdered in their beds by people they thought loved them. Others had died in agony in the hospital while everybody close to them stayed well clear."

"That's awful." I grabbed Uncle Pete's hand and squeezed it. "But people were funnier about death in the old days, weren't they? All that calling cancer the big C and only speaking about it in hushed voices."

Uncle Pete ripped his hand away, using it to lift the beer to his mouth for another big gulp. "My childhood is not 'the old days,' thank you very much. And not wanting to talk about cancer isn't the same as folks being murdered."

"Family violence is always a terrible thing," I mused, recalling a similar warning from Lucas not too long before. "But how many ghosts are we talking about here?"

"Enough. All it takes is one or two to scar a boy for life."

Uncle Pete finished the bottle and helped himself to another. Hopefully, I could drop by the superette to replenish the supply before Brody came home and discovered how generous I'd been with his favourite tipple.

"Was it just the ghosts that put you off this place? It seems to have plenty of other charms to make up for it."

"Things were always moving around. Once, the

box we used to fix toys ended up in the back garden with a giant rat inside it."

I nodded along, waiting for the phrase to make sense. After giving my brain a minute to catch up, it refused to turn out anything approaching coherence, and I had to ask, "Sorry, what box are you talking about?"

"There was a box upstairs in the attic. We'd put any broken toys inside it, leave them for a few hours, then take them out again, good as new." He ruffled the hair on the back of his neck and gave a soft laugh. "Just as well. We were rough as kids. I remember setting fire to a doll once, just to win a fight with your mother."

It didn't even come close to the things I'd done to dolls in my youth. If the poor things ever came to life, they'd spend the rest of their days in heavy counselling.

"Does it still work, do you think?"

He shrugged, chugging the last of his second beer. "I don't see any reason it shouldn't." Uncle Pete caught my eye and jerked his chin at the destroyed books. "Are you trying to avoid the library policeman?"

"It's the librarian that worries me. Patsy won't be pleased if I try to explain that 'nothing' came inside and tore her treasured books apart. Sometimes it doesn't matter if you're innocent. Being the messenger is enough."

"The box had an inlaid mother-of-pearl design on

its top," he said, linking his hands behind his head. "About a metre across and half that in depth. It looked like the old school trunks they used to have in those old English boarding schoolbooks you liked."

It had been a good ten years since I'd last read a boarding school adventure book, but I understood at once what he meant. "Are you coming?" I asked when I stood up and he stayed seated.

"To the attic?" Uncle Pete's face turned pale, and he stood up just long enough to grab another beer. "Not on your life. If you don't come back in fifteen minutes, I'll call the police and run away. There's no way I'm risking my life to repair a few old books."

"Make sure Muffin's okay while I'm searching, then." I thrust the kitten into his lap, surprising them both. "If something life-threatening happens, get her to safety."

"Don't be silly." Muffin struggled until she could jump onto the table. "Number one, there's nothing dangerous in this house now. Whatever was going on stopped as soon as you came inside. Number two, if there *was*, better two of us face it than one."

She marched across the table and leapt down beside me like a brave soldier. "Come on. Let's find this repair kit box so I can reward myself with another treat."

Uncle Pete didn't show the faintest sign of shame that he was being shown up in the bravery stakes by a kitten. He settled farther back in his chair and waved us off.

"The worst thing that could happen now is Brody returns home and finds us nosing around his room without permission." Muffin happily jumped into my arms to save her the long trawl upstairs. "Maybe we should send him a text?"

"Good idea." I composed a quick note while standing outside his door. "I can't imagine what's keeping him so long, anyway. Even if he bombed out on his mysterious job interview, he should be home by now."

"If he bombed out, maybe he went straight to the Tavern Café to pick up an extra shift."

There was no answer to my text and when I DM'd his social media account, it didn't show a timestamp for being read.

"Forge ahead?" I raised one eyebrow and looked at Muffin.

"Better to ask forgiveness than permission."

I tentatively opened the door, shielding my eyes so I couldn't see anything but the floor in front of me.

"What are you doing?" Muffin stared at me in surprise. "You can hardly search for a magical box with your hand over your face. Be sensible."

"Instead of searching, I thought I'd send out a little magic spell to do the job for me."

Muffin trotted forward with a haughty sniff.

"Magic is for helping us do the impossible when it needs doing. It's not a replacement for effort."

Okay. Fair enough.

To start with, I searched in the corner behind the silk screen where Esmerelda's clothes trunk was stored. It seemed the most likely place for a magic box to be hiding out, but in a second, I could see it wasn't there.

"Do you remember the box Uncle Pete was talking about?"

"Vaguely," Muffin said, matching her tone to the word. "But there's been a lot of stuff go through this house over the years. Esmerelda was a bit of a hoarder."

Hoping I wasn't about to see sights I'd later wish to unsee, I pulled open the wardrobe door and peeked inside. Brody's rooming style appeared to be keeping everything within arm's length of the bed—a style matched nicely to mine—and the large walk-in space was devoid of clothing.

"If I lift you, can you check the upper shelving?" Muffin agreed, and I hoisted her up to peer into the corners my height didn't allow. "Anything?"

"There's a box up here but it's small."

I pulled a chair from my room into the attic and stood on it to reach. The box was only six inches wide, but the top also matched Uncle Pete's description. "Only one way to know and that's by testing it out."

As I pulled it free, it revealed a shoebox crammed even farther back. With a grunt of effort, I stretched my fingers as far as they would go and snagged it by the corner.

"What's that for?" Muffin asked, wrinkling her nose at the musty smell.

"Treasure always hides in shoeboxes," I said as I jumped off the chair. One peek inside cured me of that hope. "Or old paperwork."

"This must be the mini version," Uncle Pete said when we brought the boxes downstairs. "I'm sure the one we had as kids was much larger."

"Hand me that beer bottle, will you?" I tucked it inside the wooden box and closed the lid. "Now, how long do you reckon this'll take?"

"Goodness knows, but if this works, I wouldn't mind taking it back home as a souvenir."

Muffin tapped the lid. "It probably won't work outside the house, so you'd have to stay in this town you hate so much to take advantage."

"Then I guess I'll settle for buying my refills." He tipped his head back and closed his eyes. "You know, I once hid in that broom closet where you found the body. When I was younger, I was a champion at hide and seek."

Muffin didn't look impressed. "Hiding in a closet doesn't sound all that great."

"I'd sneaked a small stash of my auntie's pixie dust to render me invisible if someone came looking."

"You mean, you cheated." Muffin's expression grew even sterner. "Hardly a champion thing to do."

"It is when you're young. Most kids aren't bright enough to cheat at anything." Uncle Pete shifted on the chair, sliding his thumbnail under the beer bottle sticker until he could peel it back. "While I was in there, someone started whispering to me."

The hairs on the back of my neck rose. "Who was it?"

"Dunno. They warned me that my aunt was part-demon and a murderer. When I told Mum, she dragged us out of there and we never visited again."

For a long time, neither of us spoke, until Muffin's snores broke the deepening silence.

"Your familiar's got a funny sense of timing."

"I think she's under a spell," I whispered, patches of gooseflesh bumping out along my arms. "Every time someone mentions the body upstairs, she falls asleep. I thought she was doing it on purpose but now I'm not so sure."

He sucked the last of the beer out of his bottle and slammed it on the table right by Muffin's ear. The kitten continued to dream on, oblivious.

"Uncle Pete?" My voice barely made a sound at all. "Do you remember having another Aunt? Her name was Rose."

"Who told you about her?"

"I found her birth announcement in the paper, along with Esmerelda and Dimity."

For a second, I thought he was going to tell me something, confess maybe, or give me another piece of my family puzzle. Then Uncle Pete stretched over the table and flipped up the lid of the box, making the mother-of-pearl twinkle.

"Looks like the beer's ready," he said, pulling out a full bottle, indistinguishable from the ones still stored in the fridge.

Before I could ask again, a knock came on the door. Darla Quincey stood on the porch, Reggie by her side. "Thank goodness you're home," she said, stepping inside without waiting for an invitation. "After all that kerfluffle this morning, I wasn't sure you would be."

"Nowhere else to go." I pulled the door closed behind them, satisfied the nosy neighbour syndrome appeared to have died away. "Does this mean you worked out the formula already?"

"Worked it out, took out the toxic ingredients that make the monster hunters hallucinate us as the enemy, and put it back together the way it should be." Darla thrust a plastic drinks bottle into my hand. "Go on. Have a try."

"Will it work on me?" I asked, raising an eyebrow at the thought of being a guinea pig.

"Good point. Where's a human when you need

one?" Darla pouted for a moment, then clicked her fingers. "Can't you call that nice policeman back here and have him take it for a test run? He's the one you've got the crush on, after all."

As my face turned the same shade as my hair, I heard Uncle Pete chuckling behind me. "Told you," he said with satisfaction. "This town gets a hold of you any way it can."

"How about him?" Darla asked, pointing.

"He's already a pixie so it won't work." I rubbed my eyebrow and tried to think of another suitable test subject but couldn't. "Okay. I'll give Lucas a call."

As I dialled the number, I hoped my luck was trending upward for the day.

CHAPTER NINE

"It's mesmerism," Darla explained as Reggie greeted Lucas at the door and turned him into an instantly compliant subject. He happily sat at the kitchen table without a grumble, waiting placidly for the werewolf to instruct him on what to do next. "Otherwise, this shifter would never get a girlfriend."

"Hey. I'm right here and with far more sensitive ears than you," Reggie gently remonstrated. "And it hardly looks good for you, since you're the girlfriend in question. Now, is everyone cool with what we're doing?"

"Not really." I took a deep breath. "How do I know it's safe?"

Darla picked up the bottle and took a swig. "Because I'm not self-destructive or an idiot, yet I'm happy to consume it. I can't guarantee what the effect of seeing things he's not meant to will have on your friend, but the potion won't harm him on its own."

"Told you this place was evil," Uncle Pete said, his words mushy at the edges. "I bet when you woke up this morning, you didn't think of yourself as the type of person who'd compel another to drink some weird potion. Yet here you are."

He had a point. On the other hand, Lucas fainting and losing his memory whenever the supernatural world got too in his face wasn't a great result either. I took a small sip from the bottle, risking witch cooties to reassure myself it wouldn't make him drop dead. It tasted like spring flowers dissolved in dew.

"How did you feel when you saw the supernatural world for the first time?" Darla laid a hand on my shoulder, turning me to face her. "Did it send you screaming around the bend?"

"No, but…"

But it had been gradual. My hair had changed over a few days, with my ears and face not far behind it. Seeing the twins' wings had been a privilege and hearing Muffin speak, a delight.

"It won't last forever. My estimate is the effect will last for three to four hours, tops."

Three to four hours. Not bad. I'd blown some pixie dust into Lucas's face and rendered him intoxicated for about an hour on our second meeting. Not knowingly, of course. That was the main difference.

"Can you unmesmerise him?"

Reggie flicked his fingers. "The dude is back in control."

Lucas frowned at the table, then peered around him. "Sorry. I've lost track of the conversation. What were you saying?"

"This is a special liquid," I said, pushing the bottle towards him. "If you swallow it, you'll be able to see some things we can't otherwise explain to you."

He smiled at me, flashing his straight, white teeth. "I've missed something, haven't I?"

"You're missing something all the time," Darla said, tapping her foot. "This will ensure you don't do that anymore."

"It's harmless. I've tried it myself." My forefinger prodded the bottle a little closer. "Go on."

Lucas scanned the faces surrounding him, losing some of his grin. "No, I'm still not getting it. What's going on?"

Uncle Pete sighed. "Look, mate. There's an entire world of supernatural beings you can't see and it's harming your ability to solve crime in this area. Take a swig from the bottle and you'll have your eyes open. Presuming it doesn't send you stark raving mad, you'll become a better officer."

"Right." Lucas stared at the bottle. "Yeah, I'm not getting you."

"Drink. The. Bottle." Uncle Pete punctuated each

word with a slap on the table. "Just a sip to start with." He waved his hand wildly in the air. "Join the club full of freaks. It's fun."

"One of us," Darla and Reggie chanted under their breath. "One of us."

"I get that you're trying to peer pressure me into taking a sip of what might very well be an illegal substance," Lucas said, squinting at me. "But I'm not a teenager."

"Do it for your girlfriend," Darla said with a giggle. "Show her you're a real man."

"Right. That's it." I picked the bottle up and stored it in the fridge. "Let's stop the whole thing there. We can try something or someone else, later. I've got a pile of irreplaceable library books to put back together, then dinner with my mum."

Muffin suddenly woke with a snort. "Who decided to hold a party without telling me?"

"Everyone's leaving," I said, nodding to Darla and Reggie who were already at the door. "Thanks very much for your help and I'll be in contact soon."

They let themselves out, although Darla pouted slightly. When Lucas didn't stir, I shooed him upright. "Nice to see you again, PC Bronson. Always a pleasure."

"Wait. Wasn't I on a callout?"

"All sorted." I turned to face Uncle Pete as Lucas left. "If you go now, you should be able to find a cheap bed and breakfast before they book up for the night."

"Point taken." He got to his feet, swaying slightly. "I'll invite myself along to this dinner tonight if you don't mind." He gave a large burb and winced at the smell. "Or even if you do mind."

"Fine. Text me the address of where you end up and we'll swing by to collect you on the way."

Another second of shooing and he left, shielding his eyes from the bright afternoon sun.

"Should I leave too?" Muffin asked with a yawn as I returned to the kitchen. "Since it appears you need some quality alone time."

"I need some quality thinking time, is more like it," I said, patting her. "And you're always helpful with that."

After spending the next few minutes scraping the remainders of the library books into the box, I closed the lid and patted it. To my surprise, it had doubled in size. I opened it again, pushing more library book scraps inside, and shut the lid on a box that now took up half the tabletop.

"Here are more," Muffin said, nosing a few pages out from behind the couch. "Whatever tore those books apart, really wanted them gone."

Much as I didn't want to devote the time necessary to read through the thick volumes, seeing them destroyed made my stomach twist. "Well, hopefully, this works out and I don't have to confess all to Patsy."

"Nothing angrier than a book goblin who doesn't get her treasure back."

I placed the last few bits of paper into the box and closed the lid again. This time, the box grew so large it nudged the shoebox off the table. Receipts and dockets sprayed out, one slithering under the oven while another drifted halfway underneath the fridge.

With a groan, I bent over and fished them out. The paper under the oven was a yellowed clipping from a newspaper, advertising a two for one special on laundry detergent. The stapled pages caught under the fridge were old receipts for renovations to the upper floor.

"Fascinating stuff," I muttered, popping it back into the shoebox, then sweeping the rest of the loose papers in my hand. "If we ever need an extension on the house, we'll know who to call." I glanced back at the receipts, sniggering at the date on the top. "If only they weren't long dead."

"What renovations?" Muffin climbed into the shoebox to inspect the typed pages, curling up and laying her head down for an extraordinarily close view. "I don't recall the upper floor being remodelled."

"I'd tell you if you weren't sitting on them." I shooed her out of the way then flicked back the top page to reveal a set of blueprints. "It's extending the attic room and putting a false back in a cupboard."

My words caught in my throat as I stared at the faded design. The plans showed a detailed view of the closet where the dead pixie had been found.

"Right." I grabbed my laptop and went through to the lounge where I collapsed onto the sofa. "Martingale Building and Repair."

"What's the matter?" Muffin stared at me with concern. "Surely, you're not thinking about renovations at a time like this?"

"And if I ask you to explain what sort of time it is, are you going to fall asleep again?"

The question caught her mid-yawn, and she shot me a guilty glance as an answer.

"If they're still in business, they haven't discovered the wonders of the worldwide web," I declared a minute later, finding nothing online. I shut the laptop and pursed my lips in thought. "The library will have old phone books and local newspapers." I smacked my thighs and stood up. "Come on, we're going on a trip."

"Do you want me to distract Patsy while you search for answers?" Muffin chuckled. "I'd hate for her to find out what happened to her precious books while you're attempting to dig up information."

"How about we both just keep that to ourselves?" I said while locking the front door. "Until we find out if the box will solve that problem, there's no need to worry her."

"Worry her?" Muffin snorted with delight. "I don't think you've got to grips with Patsy's personality."

I ignored her amusement and quickly walked to the library. Without a sack of books on my back, it took far less time than the previous journey.

"Hello?" I called out when I found the front desk empty. "Anyone about?"

A bell sat on the counter and I hesitated with my finger over it. "Do you think I'll be able to find stuff just by looking?"

Muffin shook her head. "Not unless you've got a half-day set aside to comb through the archives." She put a paw to her mouth. "I promise I'll be good."

The loud ting emphasised the silence in the building. Apart from us, there didn't seem to be anybody using the library at all.

"Patsy," I called out when another minute passed with no response. "Are you here?"

After another pause, I walked behind the counter and opened the staff room door. Nobody was inside. A door led off to a staff bathroom, and I knocked, but that room was as empty as the first.

"Patsy," I yelled, feeling a trickle of dread drip down my spine. I headed for the back room she'd shown us earlier in the day, digging my fingers into my scalp for a shot of pixie dust. The door was locked, and I stared in dismay at my hand. No trace of dust was there at all.

"What's going on?" I spun around on my heel, suddenly certain the invisible creature of the morning was sneaking up behind me. "Why can't I create pixie dust any longer?"

Muffin jumped onto my shoulder and peered at the top of my head. She ran a claw along the side of my skull, almost hard enough to draw blood. "It's gone."

"Gone?" I scratched harder, shaking my hair out as I trawled every inch. "How can it just be gone?"

"Forget about that," Muffin cried. "Break the door down. If Patsy's in trouble…"

Her words trailed off, and I understood. We could call the police without pixie dust. Or the ambulance.

I kicked at the door, hitting it squarely just below the lock. Although it juddered, a shock that ran up my leg to my hips, the door held. As I raised my leg for another kick, I saw the key lying nearby on the floor. New fear flooded into my belly as I realised Patsy would never leave it out here.

With a quick twist of the handle, I stepped inside before my eyes properly registered what they were seeing. Every book in the room was in shreds. The spines were torn and twisted, trailing threads from old-fashioned bindings.

The minor damage that had brought the treasured

volumes into this room for repair had been obliterated in a new wave of destruction.

A level of destruction matching to the books in my house.

"Patsy!" I ran around the back of the tall shelf but couldn't spot her anywhere. There was no way the woman I'd met this morning would tolerate this damage while there was breath left in her body to fight it.

With shaking hands, I pulled out my phone. "Lucas?" As he answered I put my finger to a dark spot on the splintered door frame. Blood. "I think Patsy has been kidnapped from the library." My throat was so tight I couldn't swallow. "Kidnapped or worse."

CHAPTER TEN

I called Rosie and Posey after the police arrived. Lucas had taken a bare minimum of details before heading inside, although I'd waylaid Syd to explain the invisible creature prowling the library earlier.

"I guess it's no use keeping an eye out," he said, tipping me a wink before ploughing in after his partner.

His enforced cheer made me feel slightly better about the situation, but I was glad when the twins waved at me from along the street.

"Tell us all about it?" Rosie exclaimed, pulling me into a bear hug. "What happened? When? To whom?"

Posey stood back, frowning at the door to the library. "Patsy is a strong woman more than capable of taking someone on."

"She could just be off on a little jaunt," Rosie said, testing out a bright smile. "With no assistant, it's hard to know what to do when you're called away from your post."

"Patsy would never leave the library open." Posey rubbed her forehead and scanned the road, which was almost empty. "The number of times we've turned up to investigate some legal principle only to find a 'back in five minutes' sign." She shook her head.

"Perhaps she was in a rush."

I glanced from one to the other, feeling something was off-kilter. "Where are your wings?"

"Eh?" Rosie stroked her back and narrowed her eyes at me. "They're here, same as always. If you're playing a prank, this is hardly the time."

Posey leant forward, her face keen with interest. "Can you really not see them?"

"Not at all." I poked a finger where they should be and felt only the gentlest hint of something there, like touching the world's softest cotton wool. "And I can't get any pixie dust off my head right now. I tried inside the library and came up empty."

"Oh." Posey tilted her head and peered at me with an intensity that made my cheeks feel hot. "Your hair is looking... hm. A little flat?"

Just as she said the words, a lock of hair fell over my eye and I tucked it behind my ear. The gesture, once a daily staple, hadn't occurred in so long my muscles cried with nostalgia. "What's happening to me?"

Muffin mewed loudly from inside my jacket, and my mouth fell open in alarm. "Now I can't hear you properly, either!"

"You seem to be depixiefying at an alarming rate." Posey patted me on the shoulder. "But I'm sure it's nothing to worry about."

The assurance did nothing to quell the panic clambering up my body. "What happens if I revert completely? Do I lose my powers forever?"

I glanced at Muffin, seeking an answer, but she could only shake her head. Any words of wisdom were lost, along with my pixieness.

"Your mother said she was pregnant, didn't she?" Posey tapped the back of my hand to get my attention. "Any chance you know what flavour of baby she's having?"

I could barely swallow as the ramifications hit me. My hands were trembling so much I shoved them into my jeans pockets while staring at the ground. "She hasn't said, so I guess she doesn't know yet."

"Don't worry." Rosie drew me into another tight hug. "Even if you're no longer the youngest daughter, you'll always have a place in our community."

The words had me fighting back tears, but they also rang hollow. What good was community support if I couldn't understand my best friend? Would I never hear Muffin's voice again?

Lucas waved from the entrance of the library before joining us on the footpath. "We've done a thorough sweep of the building and can't find any trace of Patsy. A forensic team is coming in from up north to do a closer scene examination than we can manage, and we've put out an alert to all stations."

"Do you have any idea what happened?" Rosie asked, tapping her foot. "A woman can't just up and vanish."

Syd beckoned me over and I excused myself. "Most of the books targeted by whatever it was are old spell books and essays on magic practices. I'm worried something is trying to get hold of knowledge they shouldn't have and became frustrated when they couldn't."

"That doesn't sound like good news for Patsy."

"I've called in the local coven supreme to do a sweep of the library in case she can come up with any further relevant clues." He scratched his eyebrow, which was twitching. "Other than that..." Syd shrugged. "I don't suppose you can use some pixie magic to give us a helping hand."

The piece of fringe I'd tucked behind my ear fell over my face again. "I'm not capable at the moment," I admitted. "But if Brody's at home, he can use some of the dust inheritance left by Great Aunt Esmerelda to help."

"It could be important. Can you call him at work?"

I pulled out my phone and checked the messages I'd sent him earlier. Still no acknowledgement they'd been read. I pressed the number for the Tavern Café. "I'll try but I'm not sure he's there. If he is, he's ignoring all my other attempts to get in contact."

The server who answered confirmed my suspicion. "He hasn't shown up to work there today," I said, tucking my phone back into my pocket. "And he was scheduled on the midday shift."

"Anywhere else he could've gone?"

A thousand places. Each as unlikely as the last. "I can't imagine him skipping work except for an emergency. But if he was called away somewhere unexpectedly, I also can't think why he'd shut his phone off."

Lucas drifted over—the concern on his face a mirror image of mine. "This is your flatmate you're talking about?" When I nodded, he pulled out his pad. "What's the mobile phone number?"

I recited it and he read it back to me, then glanced to Syd. "We could have Doris over at the court get us the authority to ping it."

When I raised my eyebrows, he explained. "It's not like tapping his phone or anything, but it'll let us know his nearest cell phone tower if he made or received any calls today."

Syd nodded, then tapped the back of my hand. "Does he have a find-my-phone app?"

"If he does, I don't know the passwords to access it or anything." I glanced over my shoulder at Muffin who might be shouting the code out to me for all I knew. "When I get home, I'll see if there's anything stored on the laptop."

Not that Brody used it much. He preferred to use his mobile data plan than risk interrupting Muffin playing a card game.

With my worry now stoked, I wanted to search the streets but that wouldn't solve anything. Better to let the police handle things and put my energy into fixing things within my control.

"We haven't heard from him, either," Rosie said with a worried frown as I rejoined them. "I hope he's not in any bother."

It took a huge effort to move my mind onto other matters but standing by the side of the road and speculating would only waste time. I pulled out the receipts from the remodelling and showed them to Posey. "Do you remember this company at all?"

She took the pages off me, her eyes widening as the implications of the information hit home. "I'll need to check through our records to be sure, but I think we dealt with the closure of Hans Martingale's business about a decade ago. His son bought it lock, stock, and barrel, and opened under another name."

Rosie pushed forward to read over her sister's shoulder. "Oh, yes. He was a lovely old man. Bright pink hair suited him."

"The builder was a pixie?" I squeaked.

"A halfsie. Half pixie and half witch."

"But his witch half was so powerful it made up for the drawbacks of being a male pixie," Posey said, handing the papers back. "If he'd been a bad man, the world would have trembled before him, but the universe knows what it's doing. He was a gentle giant."

"A gentle, pink giant," Rosie added with a longing expression on her face.

We walked towards their law office, Muffin tagging a lift on my shoulder. Every time she gave a mew, I felt my heart break a little more at the loss of her wise and kind words. Even if she mostly chastised me about the lack of appropriate food items and my disgraceful baking skills, it was a pleasure to hear her voice.

"These are our oldest files," Posey said when we reached the office, pulling open the bottom drawer in the filing cabinet. "When we took over the business from the last lawyer, we found out Zach enjoyed keeping paper records rather than storing things on the computer. We haven't transferred them all over."

I sat on the waiting room couch while the twins

poured over the documents, setting aside those of interest. Muffin played on the floor in front of me, pouncing on a feather duster as though it had called her a rude name.

"These are all the relevant things I can find," Posey said, spreading the files out on the table. "Most of this is just related to his closing the business, but there were a few... um... supernatural things we took care of, too."

My blank expression prompted further information out of her.

"When a witch has a surfeit of powers, they can pass them on, just like the pixies pass their inheritance down through the female line. Unlike pixies, the recipient doesn't need to share familial ties."

"So, someone in Oakleaf Glade now has his powers?"

Posey nodded. "They went to Darla, goodness knows why. She doesn't put them to any use."

I rubbed my forehead, flicking back my hair as it fell lower with every passing minute. "What can they be used for?"

"My sister is being obnoxious," Rosie said, pulling a file away from Posey with a frown. "Darla's never needed to use these powers because their primary purpose is to fight rogue supernaturals. If the community can't get them under control, she summons extra strength to deal with them appropriately."

"They would've been handy against a certain vampire," Posey said with a snort. "It's not like she hasn't had the opportunity."

"One opportunity. One." Rosie raised her forefinger in case we'd misunderstood. "And he was thwarted before she had time to intervene." She got to her feet, brushing the front of her skirt. "In fact, that very case might be why she was so willing to help with the monster hunter's potion."

"You think she reverse engineered the potion to apologise for not getting rid of Ivan for me?" I rolled my eyes. "Of course, that makes perfect sense."

"Usually, she'd turn down any request like that. Darla's a very busy witch with a lot on her plate." Muffin mewed and Rosie snorted with laughter. "Yes, that's a good point. Nobody should underestimate the draw of a cute kitten familiar when asking favours from the community."

"If Hans Martingale was involved, does that mean the skeleton upstairs was a rogue supernatural?" I asked.

Rosie immediately agreed while Posey took her time to think through the answer. "He did also just build things but with the secret compartment as part of the blueprints, I'd say it was more likely than not."

I remembered how the bones had glowed with a

faint light until Reggie touched them and they collapsed. "If there was something evil being held there, it escaped this morning."

The twins turned to each other and clasped hands. "And the same thing might now have Patsy."

"And Brody," I added, my concern for his welfare racking up another notch. "We have to find them."

But Posey shook her head. "I'll tell Darla what's going on so she's prepared but there's no way we should get further involved. It's too dangerous, especially since you've lost your powers."

"Knock, knock," my mother said from the doorway, Ben eagerly poking his head into the room to look around. "We've been waiting and waiting and waiting for you to show up and take us to dinner. Finally, we took it upon ourselves to hunt you down."

Dinner? At a time like this!

But Mum and Ben didn't know what kind of time it was, and the twins were right. Without my powers, I wasn't any help.

"Sure," I said, smacking my head as though I'd forgotten. "Let's get going. We need to pick up Uncle Pete on the way."

CHAPTER ELEVEN

"I couldn't believe it when you didn't turn up," my mother said, wriggling her shoulders against the restaurant chair to make herself more comfortable. "I was telling Ben we'd better get ready right on the dot otherwise you'd be wild, then you didn't even show."

"You didn't need to tell me," Ben said in a gentle voice, signalling to a passing server for a refill on his light beer. "I've known Elisa for over ten years, remember?"

"Of course, you have, love." My mother leaned over and planted a smooch on his cheek. "And a great time they've been, too."

"What's up with you two?" Uncle Pete asked, staring morosely at the gingham tablecloth. "Since when have you been into public displays of affection?"

"You haven't told him?" Ben asked, his eyes widening.

"Needed to let Elisa know first, didn't I?" She held out her hand, twiddling her fingers so the diamond engagement ring caught the light. "We're getting married."

"After all this time? Why bother?" Uncle Pete pointed to his glass as a waitress brought over Ben's refill. "Another one here too, please."

"The usual response is congratulations," my mother said, her smile fading. "And don't you think you've had enough to drink already?"

"If I thought that, I'd stop ordering."

The siblings glared at each other across the table and Ben caught my eye with a hint of desperation. "Did you look around the town after you left my place?" I asked my uncle, my mind casting out for topics of conversation and only hooking bland.

"Nope. I don't want to see more of it than I have already."

"Nice attitude." Mum screwed up her face. "If you're not going to be pleasant company, why didn't you just stay back at the motel?"

"Because I ran out of food and drink." As soon as the waitress placed a fresh pint on the table, Uncle Pete set to work polishing it off.

Ignoring him, I turned to Ben. "What wedding plan arrangements did you work out with the twins?"

His eyes sparkled. "So many things. We've got ideas for bouquets and table settings and about five hundred different dress designs, both for the bride and her bridesmaids."

"Speaking of which"—Mum turned to me—"would you like to be one?"

"I'll have to check my calendar," I said in a vague tone, looking around at the other tables. When I caught her face collapsing from the corner of my eye, I slapped the back of her hand. "Of course, I want to be a bridesmaid. I'd be delighted."

"Good. That's one down."

"Who're you having as your best man?"

Ben seesawed his hand. "I've narrowed it down to three. Maybe four."

"Did you remember Aidan's back in Nelson, come Monday?"

"Maybe five."

"Do you think we could talk about something more serious than your upcoming nuptials?" Uncle Pete growled.

My irritation at his behaviour suddenly overflowed. "Like what? How you tried to keep my inheritance a secret until I almost lost the chance?"

My mother sat up straight. "What's this?"

"The letter about my inheritance," I said, keeping steady eye contact with my uncle. "He received the original notice and kept it secret until after the period it stated I could claim."

"Is that true, Pete?"

"What does it matter?" He flicked an angry hand at me. "You worked it out, anyway."

"Only because the lawyers had to wait out six months for probate." I sat back and folded my arms. "If I hadn't received the notice at the time I did, the whole thing would have gone to someone else."

"And what would be wrong with that?" Uncle Pete folded his arms in a mirror image of my body language. "What great things have happened since you came here? Word on the street is you've been constantly calling the police."

"But that's because—" Mum clapped a hand over her mouth while her cheeks flamed red. "Don't mind me," she muttered as we all stared at her.

"Let me guess." I shifted on my chair and forced my hands to rest in my lap. "The twins have been telling tales outside of school."

"They hinted you might have a relationship with a certain policeman," Ben said in an apologetic tone. "But we're not taking that as gospel. No way."

Uncle Pete leant forward, jabbing his finger onto the table. "You wouldn't need to have a policeman by your side if you'd stayed in Nelson."

"No. I just would've made their acquaintance when

they evicted me from the flat because I couldn't afford the rent."

"Money isn't everything." He sat back in his chair, huffing out a breath. "It's a lot better to be poor and safe than to risk your life every day just for the comfort of living in your own house."

"Oakleaf Glade isn't dangerous." I tried to keep my voice steady, but a wobble crept in as I thought of Brody and Patsy. The town felt threatening to them right this minute.

"What do you know?" My mother's voice was tinged with alarm as she reached out a hand to her brother. "Pete? What's wrong with this place?"

"Everything's wrong. The whole town creeps with evil."

Ben clapped his hands together as our meal arrived. "What a lovely spread. I'm sure any place in the country has its share of good and bad. Just look at the crime stats. According to those, every city is a den of thieves."

He picked up a fork and speared a wedge, dragging it through the aioli before popping it into his mouth, whole. "Delicious," he mumbled.

But my mother couldn't be sidetracked so easily. "Elisa. Is there something going on here that you're hiding from me?"

"I'm not hiding anything." I shook my napkin out and placed it over my lap. "Uncle Pete had a scare when he was a kid and it's twisted his view, that's all."

"Pete?"

"Don't you remember anything about this town?"

Mum shook her head, appearing nonplussed. "Sure. It's got a nice stream we used to play in, during the summer." She sat back, nibbling a chip as her eyes flicked up to the ceiling, watching memories unfold. "There was an ice cream seller near the centre of town who'd give me an extra scoop as long as no other customers were waiting in line."

"There was a man trapped in the walls of the closet upstairs because our auntie was a demon."

My hands tightened into fists and I closed my eyes, expecting something terrible to follow. Instead, my mother gave a low laugh. "Oh, you and your nightmares. Honestly. Do you remember you had that doggy nightlight until you left home?"

The teasing edge in her voice seemed to drive my uncle insane, and he thumped his palms on the table, making our meals jump. "This isn't a joke. This town is packed full of terrible things and the longer we stay here the more damage they do."

"Right." Ben reached over and plucked up my uncle's glass of beer. "You're officially cut off for the night."

"It's not the alcohol talking."

"A statement which we'd appreciate better if you

weren't so full of alcohol you're slurring while you say it."

"Can't we all just have one nice meal out together?" Mum pleaded. "We used to have a nice time as a family. I don't understand what's happened?"

"Oakleaf Glade happened. Your daughter becoming a pixie happened."

"A what?" My mother turned a perplexed gaze my way. "Is that a job? You know I support you, but is dressing up as a character really how you want to make a living?"

"Don't judge, Kayla." Ben turned up the wattage on his smile. "Is this a mascot or an acting role?"

Uncle Pete gave a disbelieving snort and pushed away from the table, upsetting my mother's lemonade glass, thankfully empty.

"Sit down." Mum's voice was filled with steel. "You don't get to cause trouble then flounce away from the repercussions."

"And what would you know about that? You can't even see what's right in front of your face."

I glanced around in dismay at the other diners, some surreptitiously watching from beneath lowered eyes, others openly staring. "Can you stop causing a scene? These are my friends and neighbours."

"That's the whole reason I'm acting this way. They shouldn't be. We cut off this portion of our family for good reason. Do you think my mother enjoyed turning her back on her sister? She did it to spare us the ill effects of this wretched place."

"No, she didn't."

Uncle Pete turned to my mum in surprise, then shook his head. "You don't understand. You were too young."

"Lord knows I loved my mother but if you think she cut Auntie Esmerelda off because of some imaginary evildoing, you're one hundred percent wrong. It was out of spite. Mum never could stand anyone else doing better than her. Remember when she pulled up all of Miss Martin's gardenias because she won first place in the St Argyle's Church show?"

"It was because—"

"Stop it." My mother also stood, matching off against her brother. "Looking at our family through rose-coloured glasses won't help anyone and I can't believe you actively tried to stop my daughter getting her rightful inheritance over some imaginary night terror you had forty years ago. This ridiculousness stops right now."

She glanced at Ben for support and he leapt up to stand by her side.

"We're expecting a child and while we'd very much like you to be part of his life, I won't hesitate to cut you off. Seems I inherited at least that much from our mother."

My mouth fell open in astonishment. Seeing the

same woman who'd let someone in front of her in the checkout queue just because they had fewer items stand up for herself was amazing. My throat tightened with pride as my hair finally completed its descent and flowed down my back.

But… Wait a minute. Hadn't Mum just said *his* life?

"I'm going to have a baby brother?"

Mum tore her eyes away from my uncle and smiled at me, clutching for Ben's hand. "We weren't going to tell anyone until after he was born, but I guess I let that cat out of the bag." She turned a wary eye back towards Uncle Pete. "Although, having a brother isn't always what it's cracked up to be."

I danced around the table to hug her just as Syd burst into the Tavern Café, a worried expression on his face.

"What is it?" I asked as he headed straight for me.

"We've got a ping on Brody's cell phone," he whispered. "Judging from the location, we'll need help to get him and Patsy out, if they're still there."

I ran a hand through my hair, feeling useless. "Without my powers, I'm not much help at all."

"If you can lend us your great aunt's stash of dust, we have someone on the way who can help."

"A witch?"

"No. A witch can use your dust but their result won't be as strong. It's another pixie. A male. He's on his way and should be here within the hour." Syd's frown grew deeper. "We'll have to hope they survive that long."

I stared at Uncle Pete until he raised his eyebrows and shrugged. "What?"

"We've got a male pixie right here," I told Syd. "It's just a matter of convincing him to do the right thing."

CHAPTER TWELVE

"They used to mine coal just south of Oakleaf Glade," Syd explained as Uncle Pete and I climbed into the back seat of the patrol car. "Nothing like they have over on the West Coast but enough to make it worthwhile. When the country introduced stricter safety regulations in the thirties, the mines shut down. Appears the cost of a dead worker was cheaper than keeping them alive."

I rubbed my stomach as it clenched with claustrophobic fear. "You think they're down an old mine shaft?"

"Somewhere around there, according to the information from the mobile company."

He paused and one glance at the worried set of his mouth told me Syd was keeping secrets. "What else did they tell you?"

"The last time Brody's phone pinged was ten-thirty, this morning."

I bent my head as I calculated how many hours had passed since then. If Brody had been taken by a rogue supernatural, his chances of being alive and unharmed dropped to almost nil with that long a passage of time.

We pulled up outside my house and I ran to collect the pixie dust. Unsure how much we'd need, I settled for bringing the entire container.

"How'm I going to be of any help if I don't even know how to use the stuff?" Uncle Pete grumbled. His attitude might be just as surly, but I was pleased to hear his words sounding more precise. The danger of the situation had sobered him up.

"Take a pinch," I told him, opening the box. "Now picture in your mind something you'd like to happen."

"I'd like to open my eyes and find myself plonked in front of the telly at home."

"Try for something that doesn't teleport you out of this situation. How about a snack?"

"A cup of coffee might help me around now."

"Good. When you have it fixed in your mind, gently blow the dust off your palm." As a mocha cloud swirled in the backseat, I made a mental note to remember this the next time I didn't want to go out early for muffins. A mental note I immediately had to correct since magic no longer applied.

"Oh. My powers." I sat up straight as a large

reusable coffee cup appeared in my uncle's hand. "The twins thought they might be because I was soon getting a new sister but according to Mum, she's having a boy."

While Uncle Pete stared at me in confusion, I flapped my hand at him. "Not you. I'm talking to Syd."

"What else have you been in contact with today?" the officer asked, the words stilted as he concentrated on the road in front of him, hard to see in the increasing dark. "Or have they been diminishing for longer?"

Both good questions. The only thing that occurred to me was the invisible creature stalking the library. I had noticed my powers flagging after that, but it didn't mean it was connected.

"Do you know of any other cases?"

Syd frowned and glanced in the rear-view mirror. "Not off-hand but that doesn't mean it hasn't happened. Since supernaturals don't tend to keep written records we have to rely on memory and anecdotes for this stuff."

I was about to ask why, then thought of Blake Stone, the so-called monster hunter who'd been unfortunate enough to be on the receiving end of a real monster. His kind knew just enough to create a potion strong enough to view supernaturals. If they had a written record of our lives, we might end up with a lot more hunters recruited to their ranks.

"Oh, that was good," Uncle Pete said as he drained the cup. "I feel more awake."

"You'll need it," Syd said grimly. "If Patsy and Brody are both being held down the old mines, it's not just a rogue supernatural creature we need to worry about. The shafts are old and there's only timber and tradition holding the ceilings up. One wrong move and we could be buried in a collapse."

My toes turned ice cold. "At least it's not raining."

As if to spite me, drizzle pattered against the windscreen.

"How much pixie dust is this?" my uncle asked, clicking his fingers when it took my attention a moment to refocus.

"A lot." I peered into the wooden box, trying to estimate while simultaneously feeling foolish. My great aunt had gone to a lot of trouble to collect the dust together and I'd added nothing to the stores. I'd blown my chances to leave a legacy behind.

"Thanks. When we're going forward into possible death, it's good to know we have 'a lot' on our side."

The sarcasm might bite but at least this was an uncle I was familiar with. "Usually, a small head scratch is enough to propel a magic spell. This looks to be around a thousand or more of those. It's powerful stuff."

"Good to know we won't run out halfway through."

"No chance." Syd slowed the car as the road turned

to bumpy gravel on hardened dirt. "I've also got a few spells up my sleeve if it comes to that. My wand mightn't be a match for pixie dust, but it's a lot better than nothing."

"Fairies," Uncle Pete said with a snort. "We used to make fun of you guys all the time in school."

"Yeah? That's how us male fairies build up our magic muscles. Grinding male pixies into the concrete playground."

They inexplicably grinned at each other in the mirror, an act that left me shaking my head. Men.

"Get ready." Syd pulled the car to a stop. "We're here."

Here didn't look like somewhere good to be. The darkening night sky probably wasn't helping but even without that added gloom, the tightly knit forest canopy did a good job of keeping out light. Even where the moon was rising over the hills, only a few fragments made it through the dense foliage.

My uncle spoke in a soft voice, "This is the Oakleaf Glade I remember."

If this had been the first scene the town presented me with, chances were I'd have a bad taste in my mouth, too. Pushing doubts aside, I slid off the back seat and forced my feet to get moving.

"The old mine is along a track somewhere around here," Syd said, scouring the ground. "Not an official path, mind. Just worn grass where people who've been repeatedly told to stay away go back and forth."

I was about to question the attraction, then remembered a teenage Elisa who would've been more than happy to endanger herself if it meant going against an adult's instruction.

"Is this it?"

Syd and I quickly crossed over to Uncle Pete, seeing a vague trail through the undergrowth.

"Must be. Here are some torches. Don't turn them on unless you need to. Once they're switched on, everyone will lose their ability to see in the dark."

I clipped mine onto a belt loop in my jeans, then followed Syd's lead as he walked along the faint path. As we progressed, the sounds of night creatures stirring in the woods increased in volume. A morepork flew overhead, its wings tracing a shadow in the moonlight.

"Slow up," Syd whispered. "I think this is it."

My eyes strained to make out shapes in the dark. I was almost up to the gaping mouth of the mine before I saw it. "Bags you go first."

"Hold on to the back of my belt," Syd instructed. "And Pete, grab hold of Elisa. We'll go single file and when I stop, you stop too. Keep your ears peeled for the sound of anyone alive in there."

Soon my ears were straining more than my eyes as

the tunnel engulfed us. A steady drip of water came out of the depths, but it was hard to hear anything else over the sound of our movement.

"And stop," Syd whispered.

As I listened for any telltale sounds, the darkness overwhelmed me. It felt like a physical substance just biding its time until it pushed into my nostrils, my ears, my mouth.

"Did you hear that?" Uncle Pete asked, jerking back.

When the echo of his voice fell away, I thought I could hear something moving far away. Over the increasingly fast-paced thump of blood through my eardrums, I couldn't be sure.

"Maybe," I whispered. "It's coming from ahead of us."

A pity, since that was the direction I didn't want to go.

Step by shuffling step we walked farther into the mine. At a fork in the tunnel, we paused again, desperately trying to catch a sound to direct us where to go.

Syd led off again, his step more confident than mine. I think we took the left-hand side but since I couldn't see my hands in the dark, I couldn't be sure.

Uncle Pete stumbled, pulling hard on my jeans and cursing. "Any chance we can use these torches now? I can't see a bleeding thing."

"Let's just try a little while longer. If we turn them on now, they'll do more to blind us than let us see ahead."

"And you'd rather wait until something awful attacks to blind ourselves?"

"Shh!"

I thought Syd was just using the command to stop Uncle Pete's whining, then I heard the sound, too. A moan from ahead. Not far away. I pushed against Syd's back to get him going again. "Should we call out to them?"

"If that's Brody or Patsy, they've probably heard us coming for ages. That means they either can't respond anyway, or we've got a nasty shock in store for us, just ahead."

I pulled the torch of its clip. Not to use as a light but as a potential bludgeon. "Do you have your dust handy?" I whispered to my uncle. If he nodded, I couldn't see him but the tug on my jeans suggested yes.

"What am I meant to picture? How will this stuff know who to target?"

"It just knows. Try to do something evil and the dust just falls to the ground."

Another groan sounded and we fell silent, intent on reaching our friends. When Syd abruptly stopped again, I wasn't prepared and ran into the back of him. "What?"

"The earth gives way here."

My stomach dropped to my knees like an elevator with a snapped cable. I stayed frozen in place while Syd searched for a way past, expecting at any moment for the ground to disappear beneath my feet. Uncle Pete's hand fell away from the waistbelt of my jeans and for a moment I felt like I was floating—untethered —in space.

Then I heard a snort right by my ear. "Uncle Pete. It's here!"

Syd whipped his wand out of his uniform trousers and waved it above his head. "Invisible creature, you are now incapacitated."

A trail of sparkles burned my retinas, leaving dancing stars floating in my eyes as it dissipated. Someone cried out in pain. I turned my torch on, aiming it towards the noise.

Brody lay on the mine floor, holding a hand up against the intrusive light. I only caught a glimpse before my watering eyes closed—blinded as much by the torch as I had been by the darkness.

"Is Patsy here, too?" I called out. When he didn't immediately answer, I cracked my eyes open a sliver and worked my way to his side. From there, I could see her, lying just beyond him. "Syd. Help me."

"We thought you were the creature coming back," Patsy gasped. "It's around here somewhere."

"How did it get you down here?" Unable to find any bonds, I helped Brody to his feet. "Are you trapped somehow?"

"We were scared to move," Patsy said, using the wall to get upright. "Where are we?"

"In the old mine shaft," Syd said, flashing his torch up and down the pair to check they were okay. "If you can both walk, we should get out of here. Being invisible is even more of an asset in the light."

"It compelled us somehow," Brody said, pressing close to me as we retraced our steps.

Patsy nodded. "Even though we were both conscious, we couldn't stop our feet from moving."

"Wait a second." I held up my hand and shone the torch beam along the tunnel. "Where's my uncle?"

A quick scan of the mine told me the answer. Not here.

Pieces of the day fitted into place, forming a complete picture. My uncle's hasty arrival in town, his hatred of the place, followed by a string of strange events.

We hastened out of the mine shaft, emerging from the dark tunnel to find the police car gone.

"Either the creature has him or your uncle is behind the kidnappings," Syd said, giving voice to my suspicions. "We'd better hustle to find him before anything worse happens."

A large knot formed in my stomach. "He has the box of pixie dust."

I'd just handed it straight to him. A gigantic present I might as well have tied with a bow.

CHAPTER THIRTEEN

"*I* told you we were in a battle," Patsy said as Brody drove us away from the old mine.

Patsy had been hijacked and forced to ride out to the site on her bicycle, a transport useless for getting more than one of us back to town. Luckily—although given the circumstances I was hesitant to term any part of this 'luck'—Brody had been in his vehicle, driving home when the creature struck.

"Did you read through those books I gave you?" she asked. "We'll need every piece of pixie power on our side if we're going to defeat this rogue."

"You mightn't have noticed, but my pixieness is on a downhill slide at the moment." I touched a hand to my hair. My back had grown used to it standing upright and the weight of it on my shoulders now felt uncomfortable.

"What did you do?"

I shrugged. "Rosie and Posey thought it might be because my mother was having another child, but she says the ultrasound showed a baby boy."

"Hm." Patsy's nostrils pinched together as she stopped glaring at me and faced forward. "Maybe the child was lying the wrong way."

Syd chuckled. "My knowledge of obstetrics isn't vast but from anatomy class, I'd venture that mistake only happens in reverse. A boy might be misidentified as a girl in the womb, but not the other way around."

"It could be the cord," Patsy snapped. "And even if you're not operating on full volume, there must be some of your magic left."

"It doesn't matter," I said, scratching a fingernail across my scalp and coming up empty. "Without access to another source of pixie dust, I'm out of fuel."

"You didn't answer my question," Patsy said after a moment of silence. "Did you read those books?"

"Something tore them apart," I admitted in a soft voice. "My kitchen looked as bad as your library."

Patsy clicked her tongue and folded her arms. "So we've got no magic, no knowledge, and no hope of stopping your uncle. Tell us again why we're heading straight into the lion's den?"

"We have to try," Syd said in a grim voice. "And I've still got my magic."

"Didn't stop Uncle Pete fleeing the scene, so I'll chalk that one up in the useless column."

Patsy's logic clicked home. "Maybe we should build up our army before we go headlong into a fight," I said. "The twins told me Darla has the power to stop a rogue supernatural. We should collect her if we think my uncle is the true culprit."

Syd turned to frown at me. "Does that mean you have doubts?"

I rubbed my eyes, still sensitive from the rapid light changes in the mine. "What time did you call him about the body in the cupboard?"

"Lucas rang all your family members after we got back to the station." Syd closed his eyes and wrinkled his nose. "That would have been nine o'clock, or around then."

"And what time did you get taken over, Brody?"

"An hour after that, at least. My interview didn't start until nine-thirty."

"What?" I sat back in my seat. "But you left home well before then."

"Because I wanted to prep all the potential questions without an audience." He lifted his shoulders. "You and Muffin are great and I'm sure you would've been supportive, but I just wanted the chance to clear my head and focus."

"There's no way my uncle could've made it down from Nelson in that space of time. It's over five hundred kilometres. Even if he pulled a Lundy three hundy, it wouldn't put him in town until long after midday."

"A what?" Patsy hooked an eyebrow at me.

"Let's just say speeding," Syd said, waggling a finger at me. "And I don't think he was in Nelson. Your mother gave us a contact in Windwhistle, near Mt Hutt. If he put his foot down, he'd have been here in an hour, easy."

"How did he get so powerful?" Playing devil's advocate was easy, considering how devastated my mother would be if our suspicions proved true. "Uncle Pete's always been anti-Oakleaf Glade and Esmerelda's side of the family. I can't imagine him going rogue."

"You don't have to imagine," Patsy snarled. "You saw for yourself."

"No, I didn't. I was too focused on Brody and you to see anything else."

"If we get there, and he's got a perfectly rational explanation, that's fine." Syd caught my eye and held it. "But I don't think it's likely."

"Even if it's just that the creature got hold of him," Brody said, "I think we have to prepare ourselves for a fight. If it's inhabiting him, you'll feel like you're fighting your uncle, even if it isn't truly him."

"Whatever the rogue turns out to be, I want five minutes alone with him after you've got him in restraints." Patsy's teeth gleamed in the headlights of a car going the other way.

"I'm a sworn officer of the law," Syd reminded her. "That's not going to happen."

"Hopefully, you reconsider." Patsy sniffed. "I thought I was being generous limiting it to that."

"Why does it have such a fixation on destroying books?" A sudden movement had me turning to stare out the back window, but it was just the shadow of a bat passing across the rising moon. "I mean, I'm not much of a reader either but that's taking things to the extreme."

"There's probably some ritual in an ancient volume that it's after." Given the implications of what she was saying, Patsy seemed remarkably sanguine. "Considering it's invisible, I'd imagine the creature is desperate to obtain human form."

"So, you don't think it's my uncle, either?"

She held up a hand. "I didn't say that but after having it tag a ride in my body, I'm prepared to believe your uncle took on board a hitchhiker rather than being the brains behind this operation."

"What kinds of supernatural beings can use people in that way?"

Patsy tilted her head to one side. "There's a few I can think of. Even my fellow goblins can take over a body for short periods if they need to."

"But surely a goblin wouldn't destroy another goblin's hoard?"

"Not normally but this day is turning out to be anything but normal." Patsy leaned her head against the window, staring into the darkness outside. "On the other hand, a goblin has its own physical form to return to after a joyride. This rogue doesn't seem to have anything like that."

"Are there supernaturals who are usually invisible?"

"Only if they give up their physical form." Patsy flapped a hand with impatience. "No. This is all idle speculation and isn't doing anyone any good. Let's just stick with what we know. Your uncle disappeared in the middle of a rescue mission and absconded with the town's largest single stockpile of pixie dust. Whether that's down to him being the rogue, or being used by another, we need to focus on finding and disabling him."

Although the pronouncement made my throat hurt, the librarian was right. I turned my attention back to the road, tapping Brody on the shoulder when I saw Darla's turnoff.

"Let me do the talking," Syd said, a suggestion we all promptly ignored as we piled out of Brody's car.

"Darla? Are you home?" I called out before we even knocked on the door. The lights inside showed she was, and soon enough Reggie answered my call.

"Haven't you caused enough trouble for one day," he scolded, the ferocity of his expression catching me off guard.

"Trouble? What trouble have I caused?"

Darla pushed Reggie aside and sighed. Since I'd last seen her, the witch appeared to have aged twenty years. Her eyes stared out of dark circles and the lines around her mouth and eyes had etched deep into her skin.

"What's happened?" I reached out a hand, which Reggie batted away.

"It's the silly formula you made us cook up." His upper lip curled in a snarl and I backed up a step, my heartbeat quickening. "Darla took a sip to show you it was harmless and now look at her!"

"Have you lost your powers?" Syd asked in a small voice. When Darla nodded, he turned a strained face towards me. "The potion must have stripped you both of your magic."

"Both?" Reggie stared at me, tipping his head to one side as he took in my hair and rounded chin. "You've lost yours, too?"

The implications thudded home. "If neither of us has any power, how are we going to confront my uncle?"

"We're not." Patsy was already halfway back to the footpath. "I'm not having any part of this. The creature took me on one joyride and I'm not about to let it take me on another."

She turned on her heel and fled, melting into the darkness.

"Well, that's a goblin showing her true colours," Reggie said with a hint of derision. "They're always after the treasure and never want to fight the battle to win it."

Who could blame her? I looked at Brody, a male pixie without magic of his own. Syd, a fairy with a wand only capable of small feats. Reggie was our best bet.

"Can you change without the benefit of a full moon?" I asked him.

"Sure," he said. "But it'll just turn me a lot hairier. I can tear a small rabbit to shreds but I'm powerless against magic and if my opponent is bigger, you can count me out."

"What about your mesmerism?"

"It works great against humans. Is this thing human?"

Syd seemed to be weighing up our options, too. "We can pick up the twins. Three doses of fairy magic are better than one."

"How much better?"

He stared at me for a long while, not answering. "If I can slap a pair of supernatural cuffs on him, that'll negate his powers."

"Elisa!" a voice called out behind me. I turned in astonishment to see Ben and my mother standing on the footpath, waving. "Fancy running into you. We were just taking the long way back from the restaurant."

"M-mum." My brain stuttered to a stop along with my mouth. Visions of horror crowded into my head. "You can't be here."

"Nonsense," Ben said with jovial equanimity. "This is a free country and we can go anywhere we please. Can't we babe?" He squeezed Mum's shoulder.

"Elisa's right," Syd said, stepping forward. "We're involved in a dangerous situation and can't have civilians accidentally wandering into the line of fire."

"Are you talking about guns?" My mother's voice was terrified.

"Just a figure of speech," Syd assured her. "But it's too dangerous to stick around here."

"If it's too dangerous for me and my soon-to-be-wife, then it's too dangerous for Elisa," Ben declared, moving over to take my arm. "Come on. If I'm going, you're going too."

"No, I have to stay here."

"You do what your father tells you," my mother scolded before whirling on her heel to point a finger in Syd's face. "And you should be ashamed of trying to take my little girl into an unsafe situation. What gives you the right?"

I held my hands up. "Nobody is making anybody do anything," I said. "We've just got something to take care of and it doesn't involve you, okay?"

"No, it's not okay." Now I was the recipient of the pointed finger. "Whatever you've got yourself caught up in, we're here to support you."

"I'd rather you stayed out of it."

"That's not your call." Ben puffed out his chest. "Just tell me what to do, officer. I'm ready to assist."

"You can't. You're not magic."

"You'd be surprised," Ben said, then his face twisted with confusion. "And who needs a magician at this time of night?"

"Please, can you just take Mum home?"

"If you're staying here, Elisa, then we are too." My mother folded her arms and raised an eyebrow at Syd. "If you want us to leave, then you'll have to arrest us. Is this something to do with my brother?"

My mouth fell open as I stared at Mum. How had she guessed? As though reading my thoughts, she gave a single nod of her head. "Pete was always babbling on about how Oakleaf Glade was full of demons and monsters and pixies wielding their evil magic spells. My parents might never have paid him any mind, but I know when my brother's lying, and he certainly thought he was telling the truth."

Syd and I exchanged a glance. I tried to swallow

but a large lump stuck in my throat. "Uncle Pete might be involved," I said in a small voice.

"Ha! I knew it. All that talk tonight at dinner was just skirting around the facts. Pete never gets drunk unless he's on holiday, or he's scared. Now, what exactly are we dealing with here?"

I shrugged my shoulders at Syd, uncertain of what to do. The policeman gave a tired sigh and rubbed the back of his neck.

"It's a long story," Darla called out from the doorway. "But why don't you come inside, and we can sort it out in comfort rather than yelling at each other in the street."

"Who's yelling?" my mother said, immediately heading inside. "I wasn't yelling."

"You weren't," Ben said, a hand on her back as though steering her. "But I wouldn't mind a sit-down. My feet are plumb worn out."

When we were gathered indoors, Syd quickly ran through the events of the day, skipping our trip to the coal mine after I caught his eye and shook my head. Even without that added terror, my mother's eyes widened, and she clutched onto Ben's hand hard enough for him to wince. Still, despite hearing a load of events I would have called insane before coming to Oakleaf Glade, she didn't interrupt.

At the end of the summary, she bit her lip and stared at the ground. "It's a lot to take on board," she finally said. "But if anyone can talk Pete down with no need for magic powers, it's me."

"No." Ben put a firm hand on her shoulder. "It's time I stepped up and protected you and the baby. I'll go."

My mother stared at her fiancé as if he'd gone insane. "Well, of course, *you're* coming along. I didn't mean I'd turn up and try to talk him out of whatever he has planned on my own."

Caught on the back foot, as he often was, Ben soon slipped into the rear seat of the car, while my mother talked Brody's ear off, trying to find their common relatives. Though it didn't seem the right time to dig into our family tree, I was happy she had something to distract her. My stomach was churning, and my knees were turning into jelly.

Syd and I set off on foot, and I phoned through to the twins for extra support. Posey answered, her voice more animated than usual. "Guess who we found?" she called out before I could get more than my name out. "Rickie Martingale. He only lives half an hour up the road and was more than happy to visit us."

"Hans Martingale's son?" My voice came out sharper than usual and Syd's head jerked around, ears perking up. "Does he know anything more about the cupboard?"

"Better than that," Rosie said, breaking into the call.

"He remembers the precise reason it was built and who the pixie was."

I relayed the information to Syd who plucked the mobile out of my hand. "We need you to meet us at Elisa's house. Bring Rickie with you. We've got a situation."

When he handed the phone back to me, the twins had rung off. "Well, who was it?"

"Nobody you know," Syd said in a curt voice. "But I think I understand more of what's going on here."

We turned the corner onto my street, and I stopped dead in my tracks. "What's Lucas doing there?"

He stood outside my house, dressed in his uniform, peering up at the top storey where the lights blazed. I broke into a run, my mouth as dry as cotton wool. Syd overtook me within three house lengths but still couldn't reach his partner before he disappeared inside the front door.

"Wait," Syd called from a standstill at the gate, grabbing for my arm as I sprinted past.

I easily shook him off, my body galvanised by adrenaline. Inside, Lucas had already climbed the staircase. "Stop."

He spun around, reaching for the baton on his waist. When he saw it was me, he dropped his arms to his side. "The station received a call from a concerned neighbour," he said, taking one step back. "What's going on?"

I didn't have the breath to answer and mount the stairs, so I just held up one hand and kept coming. On the landing, I saw my uncle sat on the floor inside the spare room, the box of pixie dust open beside him.

"Uncle Pete, you need to stop."

A multitude of footsteps sounded from the storey below as the cavalry arrived en masse. Their arrival made me braver, and I stepped into the room. Blue and white police tape sagged near the floor but the cupboard—which had been in splinters—looked good as new. Through the open door, I could see the false backing. Not even the faintest mark showed where Reggie had torn it apart with his bare hands.

My uncle turned his face to me. It was streaked with tears. Pleading.

"I've been haunted by the man trapped in the walls since I was a boy. I thought I could use this stuff to get him out. Finally, free him." He lifted a handful of the pixie dust and let it run through his fingers.

"But there's no one here." He turned a forlorn face towards the cupboard. "I think the man in the walls is dead."

CHAPTER FOURTEEN

*I*t took me a few seconds to grasp the situation. "Wait? You came here of your own accord? Nobody is controlling you at the moment?"

My uncle's baffled face was enough of an answer.

"Don't worry," I yelled downstairs. "False alarm."

"What false alarm?" Uncle Pete staggered to his feet and moved to join me. "Who are these people?"

"Pete." My mum pushed past Syd and ran up the stairs, throwing herself into her startled brother's arms. "I'm so glad you're okay." She pulled back to study his face. "You are okay, aren't you?"

He wiped the last of his tears away. "I'm fine. Just embarrassed to be caught at a bad time."

"What did you think you were doing, scaring your niece and me half to death?"

"And why did you leave the mine?" I demanded, regaining some indignation now that the immediate threat was gone. "We thought you'd been possessed by an evil supernatural creature."

Mum forgot about her brother as she turned to me in horror. "Did you go into the abandoned coal mine?" She slapped my arm. Not hard enough to hurt but enough to sting. "I swear, you'll be the death of me."

"It was perfectly safe," I lied, then pointed to Syd. "A policeman was with me the whole time."

"That was my fault," Brody said, pushing his way forward. "I was kidnapped by—" His eyes slid to Lucas. "Well, something."

"Great." My mother folded her arms and glared. "That clears things up."

Amid the heightened emotion, I was glad to see Syd pull his partner aside to chat. A few seconds later, Lucas headed out the door, shooting me one forlorn glance before leaving.

"I'm sorry to put everyone to such trouble." My uncle hung his head and sighed. "Over the years, the thought of a man being trapped in this house has weighed heavily on me, but I guess I made the whole thing up."

"Rubbish." Mum slung an arm around his waist. "If you say something in the walls of this house talked to you, then it did." She turned to me. "What happens now? Do you have an exorcist on tap?"

"Now we stop for a breath, have a snack, and let Rosie and me tell you all our news," Posey said in a firm voice. "First, we have to introduce you to Hans Martingale's son, Rickie, and you all need to listen to what he has to say."

We trooped downstairs, and I put the kettle on while Muffin padded through at the sound of a bakery bag being opened. "What are we celebrating?"

I blinked in astonishment. "I can hear you!"

Mum stared at me with a puzzled expression. "Eh? Have you been deaf up to now?"

"No, I can…" My excitement trailed off as I tried to think how to explain it.

"Muffin is Elisa's familiar," Uncle Ben said, picking the kitten up. "So they can understand each other when they talk."

"My powers must be coming back." I ran to the hall mirror and stared at my hair. It was definitely taking off skyward. When I scratched my scalp, a tiny glitter of dust coated my fingertips. "It's not all there yet, but it's on its way."

Darla snapped her fingers and a small spark shot out. "Me, too. I guess the potion only lasts for a few hours even when used in reverse."

"The toybox," my mother called out in a voice rich with delight. She ran her hand over the inlaid mother-of-pearl and peeked inside. "I thought this was out of a story or something. I'd forgotten it was real."

"My father made that," a middle-aged man said. He leant against the bench and I guessed he was Rickie Martingale. "He also made the house self-repairing in case of any accidents."

I clicked my fingers. "I saw that in action upstairs. Your dad also built a closet with a false back. This morning, it was in pieces but right now it looks brand new."

"That's why he's here," Rosie said, bubbling with excitement. "His father knew all about the creature Desiree and Esmerelda trapped in the walls. They decided on the design of the cupboard and the modifications to the rest of the house to ensure it would never escape."

Her face fell as she realised it hadn't worked as planned. Muffin tipped over to her side, a loud snore announcing she was soundly asleep. Darla frowned and picked her up, studying the kitten's face closely.

"What's the creature?" Syd, Brody, and I asked in unison.

"A gremlin." Rickie stepped forward, taking charge of the conversation. "He caused havoc in Oakleaf Glade many years ago and now appears to be doing it again."

"What kind of gremlin?" my mother asked, wringing her hands. "I'm guessing it's worse than something getting wet or fed after midnight."

"They're formless spirits from a different realm that don't belong in our world. When they come here, they attach themselves to the living like a parasite. Under their possession, a person can be enslaved for many years, if they're strong enough." Rickie stared around the group. "We're in luck that its long incarceration made this gremlin weak. If we can keep it from the spell to strengthen it, we can put it back where it came from."

He picked up the magic toybox and centred it on the table, removing the old books from inside. They were once again magically whole, and I breathed a sigh of relief. If we survived until tomorrow, Patsy might get her library back.

"We should be able to use this container to resurrect the pixie skeleton that previously held the gremlin."

"Was it Rose?" I asked, feeling a rush of embarrassment as six sets of eyes swivelled around to me.

Of the group, Brody seemed the most surprised. "You mean Grandma? She's alive and well and watching Shortland Street right about now."

Rickie frowned. "The bones belonged to Desiree. She passed her inheritance along to Esmerelda but on her deathbed insisted on trapping the gremlin. A spell should have kept her intact—a prison for the creature —but age must have weakened the magic. Once we trap it again, someone should take the role of guardian to ensure this never happens again."

Uncle Pete sagged against the bench. "This was the man in the wall who talked to me?"

"Who lied to you from the sound of it." Rickie put his hands on his hips. "If we're all in agreement, we need to come up with a plan. First, to lure the gremlin here. Second, to trap it. Third, to keep it prisoner."

"But…" My uncle's face was strained. "What right do we have to keep it locked up forever? How is that fair?"

"Once trapped, the gremlin can return to its natural realm if it chooses. If not, when it dies, it will be free to cross over, just the same as you or I. Until then, it'll mostly sleep. It's not the same as a man being trapped in a cage. More like a patient lying in a coma in a hospital bed."

"How did it speak to me if it was asleep?"

"Maybe your nearness temporarily woke it. Since it immediately lied to you and caused mischief, I'd think you'd be in favour of locking it up."

"Not here." I shrank against the wall. "Isn't there somewhere else we can keep it? The skeleton of a pixie doesn't worry me but knowing a malevolent creature lies within these walls will ensure I never sleep again."

"Where else?" Rickie once again turned to the group and examined everyone's face. He nodded after a minute passed with no suggestion. "Then it's settled."

"No, it's not." Darla stepped forward, her fingers crackling with energy. "Since I'm the one who'll be trapping the gremlin, I should get the final say."

"And where do you want it placed?"

Darla smiled at Rickie and a surge of electricity spiralled out of her hand. "Show us where the gremlin is?" she demanded, and the tiny lightning storm obeyed, drawing a picture in sparks.

"We should contain it in the same place it's headed right now. The library."

I CLASPED the box of pixie dust to my chest and peered between the shelves in front of me. The smell of old books crowded into my nostrils, and I tried to ignore it. No way did I want such a pleasant odour associated with such an unpleasant task.

"Can you hear that?" Brody asked, squatting next to me. He already had a handful of dust at the ready, as did Uncle Pete who waited farther along the stacks.

The snort was quiet but louder than our group of vigilantes, all trying to remain silent. Patsy stumbled as the gremlin got used to inhabiting her body again.

Darla had explained her line of thinking, back at my place. "The gremlin's only hope of increasing its power early is by using a spell or an incantation. Without one, it appears he can only move people out of the way. That must be why it tore the books apart. They didn't contain the information it needed. But it will keep looking."

"Why didn't it possess Uncle Pete when he had all the pixie dust at his disposal?" I'd asked.

Syd had fielded the query. "Because my wand might be weaker than pixie power but it's not useless. When I cast the spell to hold it immobile, it worked. We didn't realise because we were chasing after your uncle."

"It fears pixies," Darla had added. "That's why it fled the library each time you visited and left your home when you and your uncle entered."

"Just like spiders," I'd mumbled with an annoyed sigh. "They're meant to be more scared of me than I am of them, but it never feels that way."

Now, my heartbeat increased with every second and blood swooshed inside my ears. A drop of sweat trickled down my forehead, stinging my eye.

More scared of me than I am of it. More scared of me.

"Now," Darla called, and we ran out from behind the shelves, dust and wands at the ready.

Patsy stood still, staring wide-eyed around our circle.

Except it wasn't Patsy any longer. The gremlin had her in its grip.

From the corner of my eye, I saw Rickie open the

magic toybox. Desiree's skeleton rose from the opening until it stood her full five feet two inches tall.

"Gremlin. We cast you out on behalf of realm, the natural universe. Each thing in balance and all existing in harmony. Leave our friend."

The rest of us chanted along, flubbing a word or two but with the spirit of the sentences remaining intact. Patsy cringed, her shoulders curling forward. "I have as much of a right to exist here as you."

"You have escaped your given realm and deserve no safe harbour here," Darla intoned. She raised her hands, lightning streaking from her fingertips. "Return or remain trapped here until your spirit dies."

"No." The gremlin stamped Patsy's feet. "I've been locked up for ages. Can't a girl just enjoy a fun weekend before you send her back to the slammer?"

The gremlin tilted Patsy's head and forced an entreating expression on her face that made me recoil. Darla gave the faintest nod of her head and I raised my chin. Message received and understood. A picture of a prison cell rose in my mind.

"This is not your home. These are not your people. Return to where you belong or remain trapped until you die."

With a snort, the gremlin spun on its heel and made for a break in our human chain. I blew the dust from my palm, just as Brody and Uncle Pete did. A gigantic pink cloud surged forth, encapsulating the librarian's body.

"Then you have chosen." Darla sent a pulsing wave of electricity from her hands, snaring the gremlin inside it like a net. A frown deepened on her face as she lifted Patsy's body from the ground, beaming it across the library to land in front of Desiree's skeleton.

I pulled another round of pixie dust from the container and handed it out. Brody, Uncle Pete, and I stood shoulder to shoulder, then blew the dust out in a cloud.

One final shriek issued from Patsy's lungs, then she collapsed onto the floor. Desiree's skeleton glowed an unearthly pink. So bright, I had to look away.

Rickie unlocked the repair room of the library, standing back to allow Darla to guide the skeleton and its prisoner inside. With gentle care, she laid Desiree's remains on the central table before Rickie stepped forward again to lock the door.

Again, Darla's hands spurted forth lightning bolts. This time they danced a shining path around the edges of the door. Rather than fade away, the bright sparks continued to glow just as strongly. White light to seal in darkness.

The real Patsy stirred, sitting up.

"Is it done?" Uncle Pete asked in a small voice.

I flung my arms around him and pulled him into a hug. "It's done."

CHAPTER FIFTEEN

The following weekend, Darla settled back on my sofa in the lounge, wriggling around to get more comfortable. "Just remember, the potion is supposed to be used the other way around. One close call was enough for me."

"Has Syd been in contact with you yet?" I asked, kissing my mother on the cheek as I leaned over her to snag a cheese roll. "He got very excited at the thought of officers carrying it like pepper spray."

"He has." Darla teased off her sandals and wriggled her toes. "I don't know why he thinks it's a good idea. All I foresee is a generation of supernatural officers depriving themselves of powers because the canister is facing the wrong way."

My mother burst into giggles. "They should make a show about that. I'd watch it."

"You'd watch anything," Ben said, waggling his eyebrows. "Ask me how I know the final pairing of every season of The Bachelorette? If you hadn't said yes when I proposed, I'd be worrying."

"It's quality drama."

"It's a load of old cobblers."

"Fine. You can go out to the garage the next time it's on."

Ben's mouth gaped in horror. "But Tony and Belinda have a special date."

Mum turned to me, crossing her eyes. "See what I have to put up with."

Muffin strolled into the room, cased out the seating arrangements, and flopped down near the window. "Are there any muffins left, or did you hand them all out to guests again?"

"Good morning to you, too," I said, carrying one across. "Careful your gloominess doesn't put those rays of sunshine out."

"I'm not gloomy." Muffin wrinkled her nose in amusement. "I'm Emo."

"Solidarity, little sister," Darla said, raising a loose fist. "I don't wear black all the time just because it's traditional for witches."

The kitten yawned and stretched, showing off her toe-beans. "I feel like I could sleep for a month."

I shot a quick, conspiratorial glance at Darla. The witch had examined my overly sleepy familiar after our library escapade and concluded a spell had been placed on her to send her straight to sleep every time Desiree or the gremlin were mentioned. "As a familiar, it would be extraordinarily painful to know her mistress's remains were housing such a creature," the witch had explained. Together, we'd decided to leave it be.

Patsy knocked on the door, waving a basket full of scones. "Hope you don't mind the intrusion, but I wanted to drop these off as a thank you. The magic box is working on the last book, so I barely notice my lack of a repair room at all."

"It's funny how I completely forgot about that," my mother said with a nostalgic smile. "We used it all the time when we visited as children." She nudged her brother in the leg. "Since someone thought the way to win any argument was to pull off a doll's head."

"That's a perfect example of selective memory at work," Uncle Pete said, tipping a wink to me. "I distinctly remember pulling arms and legs off did the treat just as well."

I raised a coffee mug to Patsy, and she gave an eager nod. "That'll go down a right treat. My muscles feel like I've run a marathon just walking to work in the morning."

"Hopefully, that'll fade in the next few days," Darla called out. "But if it doesn't, hit me up. I think I might have a cure stashed away."

"Yoo-hoo," Rosie and Posey called from the doorway. "Hope you don't mind more company."

"The more the merrier," my mother declared, standing and pushing Ben until he did the same. "Have a seat."

"Shouldn't you be the one resting?" Posey said with a quick nod to my mother's stomach.

"I wish." She groaned while stretching her back out. "Apparently, things have changed since I had this one." Mum jerked her head at me. "Then it was all 'rest up for the big day,' and now it's all, 'exercise to get your body ready.' I know which recommendation I preferred."

"Let me guess," Rosie said, squinting at me. "You've been hitting the potion before you go out on a date."

I blushed and checked my hair in the mirror. Halfway down my shoulders already. Soon, I wouldn't be able to hear Muffin talk. "It's not really a date. Just a ride out to the beach."

"With a picnic lunch," my mother added. "And it took her three goes to find something suitable to wear."

With nervous hands, I smoothed the front of my sundress. "It's just hard to dress for this changeable weather."

The group turned to stare out the window at the blue sky and sunshine.

"Yeah," Ben said, pulling a face. "Difficult."

"I don't understand why you don't make Lucas take the formula," Darla said. "That's what the potion is designed for."

"Making Lucas into a human guinea pig isn't something I'm keen on. Not unless he lasts longer than my previous boyfriends."

"Ha!" My mother raised a hand in victory. "You said, *boyfriend*. I knew it." She elbowed Ben in the side. "Remember that last one up in Nelson. Trent, was it?"

"Didn't even make it to three weeks before you declared he breathed too loudly."

My mouth fell open as everyone laughed. "Well, he did."

"And Gregory. What was the complaint with him again?"

My mother's eyes were sparkling with such mischief I just had to close my eyes and wait for the roast to be over.

"He liked tomato sauce on his steak," Ben said with glee. "And Matty?"

"Had Velcro on his sneakers instead of shoelaces." Mum was laughing so hard now, she had to hold her sides.

"Only three-year-olds have Velcro," I protested, folding my arms. "A grown man should know how to tie his shoes." Ben opened his mouth, and I raised a finger in warning. "How is the wedding preparation coming along? Remember the bit of the ceremony when the celebrant asks, 'If anyone knows of any reason…?'"

"Good point." He mimed a zipper closing his lips, then immediately launched into speech again. "We'll need to strip that out, I think. Nobody needs the general public weighing in on our decisions."

"Note it down." Mum grinned, and I buried my face in my hands. "Make sure the entire ceremony is Elisa-proof."

Reggie and Brody sprinted up the path, having been for a run together. It was good practice, given the job interview my cousin had been stressing over was as a personal trainer at Oakleaf Glade's one and only gym.

Unlike his role as a server at the Tavern Café, it was guaranteed I'd never encounter him on the job again.

Totalling up the number of people inside, even my extraverted soul clamoured for solitude. Maisie floating through the wall didn't help matters, especially as she began recounting an amusing anecdote to my mother, who didn't even know the ghost was there.

"I might pop upstairs and change," I said, inching towards the staircase.

"Bags the shower," Reggie said, flying past me and claiming the bathroom as his spoils.

"Don't change again." Mum grabbed hold of my

hand and pulled me over to stand beside her. "Tell me more about this young man you're seeing."

"So you can make fun of him sometime in the future?"

"Only if the situation demands it," Ben said with a chuckle. "Hey, Brody. Can you explain to me again where you are on the family tree? I'm tasked with sending out wedding invitations."

"Well, there's my grandmother." Brody gave me a wink. "Who, despite Elisa's claims to the contrary, is not the youngest daughter of her family and definitely isn't dead."

I shielded my eyes for a second, counting back from ten. "It seemed a reasonable assumption."

"Hurtful, you mean. My poor Nana."

"How was I meant to know your Nana Ramble was actually Rose Spicer? Nothing about that name tells me anything useful. My pixie magic showed me my great aunt's grave. I didn't know Desiree had a plaque commemorating her there, as well."

"You knew I didn't come from your side of the family and that Esmerelda didn't have any children. Surely, a process of elimination would have landed you in the right place?"

Ben jumped to my rescue. "It was a very stressful time," he said in a measured voice. "I think there should be a town ordinance that insists upon nametags when you store dead bodies inside your walls."

It was hard to agree or disagree with that statement, so I opted for silence. Soon enough, Brody and Ben walked away, chatting about who should make it onto the invitation list.

My phone beeped, and I'd never felt so grateful to have an excuse to leave. With a smile, I read Lucas's quick message, then sent him a text asking him to wait outside. The last thing I wanted was for him to walk in through the front door and be ambushed.

"Gotta go." With a quick wave, I hightailed it out the door on a wave of protests and increased my walk to a jog when I heard footsteps following me outside. I gestured to a surprised Lucas to keep the engine running and lunged for the door handle. "Go. GO!"

Once we'd turned the corner, I sighed in relief and sank back in the passenger seat.

"Are you embarrassed about your family or me?" Lucas asked, wrinkling his nose at me.

"Neither. I've just had my fill of friendly advice for the day. Maybe later we can go through the awkwardness of introductions."

"It might be much later," Lucas warned, giving me a sideways glance. "The day is hot, the sea is warm, and I know every ice cream vendor at the beach by name."

"Sounds wonderful."

He gave me a lazy smile and reached out to twist a

curl of my hair around his finger. A tingle of excitement zapped across my skin and nestled in my belly. "You know, you really suit having your hair down."

I patted it self-consciously, then wound the window a fraction to let the wind catch at its length. "That's good." I caught his hand and gave it a kiss before releasing it back to him. "Because I think I might wear it this way more often."

Even with a further ten-minute drive to reach the ocean, I could taste salt on my tongue. Since arriving in Oakleaf Glade, I'd revelled in discovering about my pixie heritage, and putting my magic to good use.

Still, after an adventurous month, having a break from my strange new world felt overdue. Good company, sand, surf, and no supernatural abilities sounded like the perfect day to me.

Willow Mason is the author of Witchy (and Pixie) Paranormal Cozy Mysteries.

She lives in a small town in New Zealand, far too close to the beach and fantastic walking trails to get nearly as much work done as she should. Until someone bestows magic powers on her, she'll just keep hoping for the invention of self-cleaning dishes and self-washing clothes.

www.willowmason.com

Made in the USA
Coppell, TX
03 June 2020

26900778R00100